amaranthine chevrolet

amaranthine chevrolet

a novel

DENNIS E BOLEN

RARE
MACHINES

Publisher: Meghan Macdonald | Acquiring editor: Russell Smith
Cover designer: Laura Boyle
Cover image: Field: unsplash/Paul Nyarko; Sky: unsplash/Linhao Zhang

Library and Archives Canada Cataloguing in Publication

Title: Amaranthine Chevrolet : a novel / Dennis E. Bolen.
Names: Bolen, Dennis E. (Dennis Edward), 1953- author
Identifiers: Canadiana (print) 20240424050 | Canadiana (ebook) 20240424107 | ISBN 9781459754775 (softcover) | ISBN 9781459754782 (PDF) | ISBN 9781459754799 (EPUB)
Subjects: LCGFT: Fiction.
Classification: LCC PS8553.O4755 A81 2025 | DDC C813/.54—dc23

We acknowledge the support of the Canada Council for the Arts and the Ontario Arts Council for our publishing program. We also acknowledge the financial support of the Government of Ontario, through the Ontario Book Publishing Tax Credit and Ontario Creates, and the Government of Canada.

Care has been taken to trace the ownership of copyright material used in this book. The author and the publisher welcome any information enabling them to rectify any references or credits in subsequent editions.

The publisher is not responsible for websites or their content unless they are owned by the publisher.

Printed and bound in Canada.

Rare Machines, an imprint of Dundurn Press
1382 Queen Street East
Toronto, Ontario, Canada M4L 1C9
dundurn.com, @dundurnpress

For my mentors:
Jimmy, Norman, John, Herbert
Seb, Chris, Merv, Jack

Sorry Is Just a Word

HE DROVE STEADY TO THE THISTLEBOUND TOWN.

Steering careful past letter-faded business windows, noting a particular "Back in Ten" sign, he pulled between a truck face-out and one face-in.

The door of the dark hotel clicked behind him.

Through an archway he strode and then along the deep-tread lobby path to the diner part where two of eight tables were occupied and one man sat face-away at the counter gazing at his mirror reflection.

He slung a leg over the Naugahyde stool. Hi, Mister Teller.

A sidelong look at the boy. Young fella. A glance out the windows. Driving Jimmy's truck?

Yup.

Not licensed yet, are you?

Nearly, sir.

Thing's not two years old. What's Jimmy doing letting you take charge of it?

He can't drive anymore.

Well I don't imagine so but neither can you. Teller lifted his coffee cup. Town isn't that dead.

I'll park it. Soon as I get back to the place.

You best.

The apron-stain waitress came by. Having anything? Coffee?

No thanks, ma'am.

She wiped hands and moved off.

Teller head-gestured to the street. Mountie drove through yesterday. Might again today.

I have to take my chances.

Whyever for? Isn't Sam helping out?

Sam took off.

Did he.

Got tired of not being paid.

Understandable. But too close to harvest to be honourable.

Harvest'll have to be hired. We were going to anyway.

I suppose.

Sam knows I can make out for myself.

I suppose you can. But you're not legal to drive.

I have to get to the clinic.

Jimmy still there? Thought they sent him to the city.

He wouldn't go.

Heh heh. That's Scott all right. Teller paused to look out windows and drink coffee. Damn. Going out like this. Relatively young man.

They warned him it might get rough.

Might as well tell the gophers.

You know him pretty well, Mister Teller?

Since he was less than you.

He requested me to come and ask about something.

He did, did he ... Requested. Teller set his cup down. What about?

A personal favour.

Oh?

That's how he said it.

For who? Him or you?

Me, I guess. Or us maybe.

I don't know you too well, son.

You know I've been helping him a few years now.

Yes.

He says he thinks pretty high of me.

If you don't say so yourself ha ha.

I don't know what else to tell about it, sir.

Why don't you just get to what you're here for?

I need a favour.

You do, do you?

Jimmy says I deserve one.

He does, does he? Well, you being a fit young fella ... Teller turned his stool to inspect the boy more closely. ... I suppose a favour to you would at least be more in substance than a favour to a dying man. He shook his head. Poor old Jimmy. How long's he got anyway?

No way to tell, sir. The boy looked away to break the man's fixed eye-hold. Doctor won't say.

Hmmm. Teller finger-tapped the Arborite. Well. What then is this personal favour I can do you on Jimmy's behalf?

We need to get the forty-two registered.

The what?

Jimmy's old pickup in the barn.

Oh. Chevrolet was it?

I was driving it on the fields but now he wants it back on the road. A sentimental thing I guess. Took care of it all these years.

He got it running?

Took him about an hour.

From up on blocks?

Had it under a tarp. He's some mechanic.

Musta packed the cylinders with oil. Put new wiring in. Plugs. Points. Condenser.

All of that, sir.

Jimmy bailed me out when my Buick gave up in a blizzard near his place one time. Late fifties it was.

Jimmy'd help anybody anytime anyhow.

It's the prairie way, son.

Yes, sir.

But what would he want on his deathbed in this year of nineteen sixty-seven with a beat-up twenty-five-year-old Chevrolet half-ton he's had stored in a barn for years all registered up and ready to go?

Not sure myself, sir. But it seems to mean something to him.

And you promised you'd see to it, eh? Said you'd roll it up outside his clinic room and let him look at it one last time through the window?

Something like that maybe.

Well … Teller gazed once more into the mirror. If that's truly what he wants us to do then there's not much other than to do it. I got the forms in the office.

Can you let me have them?

I can help you fill them out ready for Jimmy to make his mark on them. That is if he's still making sense. He is conscious isn't he?

Last I saw.

Well he better. Otherwise it all goes into trust and likely to stay there a long time. Pending whoever comes up with a will or steps in to make a claim or otherwise identifies themselves as a relative or heir. He has a son for god's sake. I told him a dozen times to come in and set his affairs straight. Instead, now ... He's got an eager adolescent driving his vehicles illegally and running around with putative power of attorney trying to get things formalized last minute. Teller drained his coffee cup. Shoddy.

He's not one for rules and regulations, that's for sure.

Hell rules and regs are everybody's bane but you have to see to the tangible necessities.

I'm sure you're right, sir.

Jimmy knows I'm right. Always did but never listened.

I think he'd listen now, sir. I think he's in a listening mood.

He's still in a bed at the clinic, you say?

Yup. Got a private little room and everything.

Well. I guess a real friend would.

If we could get this paperwork done, I'd sure appreciate it for Jimmy's sake.

Yeah ... Teller stood and dug for coins in his suit pocket. Okay. Let's go across the street.

They trekked the wide windy streetspan, dodging a rolling Russian thistle. Teller opened his storefront door and flicked the CLOSED sign to OPEN.

Come and sit yourself down. Robin, is it?

Robin Wallenco, sir.

Of that Wallenco family used to live out toward Arbuthnot?

I'm told. Never met them myself.

Well I did ... Teller settled into a swivel chair and pulled at a low desk drawer. Long time ago. And now Arbuthnot itself nary exists.

I wouldn't know, sir.

Well I do know ... He plopped a worn leather journal on the desk and met Robin in the eyes. Take a good hard look at these little towns, son. Remember them while they're still here. They're a thing of the fast-approaching past.

Yes, sir.

The family heritage of a lot of people is disappearing.

It seems so, sir.

You likely have kin buried nearby.

I do.

Any other family living or otherwise?

Not around here. My dad sent me out to help Jimmy.

And your dad is where now?

The coast.

The coast. But he was from these parts.

Yes, sir. But gone away a long time ago.

I probably never met him but I knew some others of the clan. Ended up out west you say?

Went during the war. With his dad. All the way to the coast and stayed.

I knew of his father. Your grandfather. He wasn't around long either as I recall. Haven't heard of him in decades.

We don't see much of Granddad. Lives somewhere near Winnipeg now.

Teller rummaged in another drawer. Want a cookie? He proffered a tin with a wavering hand.

No thanks.

Teller took one himself and bit down. They're pretty darn good cookies. Belgian.

I'm full up, thanks.

You don't turn down cookies as good as these.

If you really want me to, sir. There was a notable joyousness in the man's shortbread crunch-munch that oddly eased Robin's mind. He picked a biscuit. I'm glad you like them so much.

Never know when you might run out of cookies. *Munchcrunch.* The Depression was like that.

No cookies?

Not a darn one. Not around me anyways. For years and years. Lard sandwiches on hard bread. Smeared-up eggs from the coop three times a day. Ground wheat. Flaxseed.

That all sounds like plain good-enough food.

Oh we never went hungry. Not much. But there weren't any cookies. Cake neither. Nor white bread.

Well everybody seems to sure make sure they keep lots of that stuff around now.

Ever since the war and prosperity there's been no shortage. Teller finished his cookie and gazed at length through his office window.

The pause lasted long enough to cause Robin an uncomfortable shift in his chair.

Teller finally shook his head and turned back to Robin. Sure seems strange to be spending good money to put a derelict farm vehicle back on the road.

It's in pretty fine shape, sir.

Jimmy's a master tinkerer, sure. But you don't hear of too many grain growers being antique enthusiasts.

Like I said. This truck is a sentimental piece for him.

Farmers round here have no time for sentiment. Hobbies. Diversions. Eccentricities of any kind. Teller's eyes had turned hard. Not this time of year anyway.

I'm sure everything's okay.

Oh you're sure, are you?

All I'm doing is what I've been told.

Uh-huh … so you say. Teller swivelled to grasp a sheet of paper from a slot in the wall. But very well. He turned back to the boy. You have the chassis and engine block serial numbers?

Robin pulled papers from a back pocket.

Ah good. Teller applied reading glasses to unfold the documents and peer at the figures. After a moment he handed them back and slid a government form across the desk. You write them in there and the name. Teller pointed with pen at paper. Here and here ... both sides. This is where you get Jimmy to sign. Or put some kind of mark.

Okay.

Teller sat back. You fairly know what you're about here. Don't you, lad?

I'm just doing what Mister Scott asked me to do.

And going about it with no little sense of pointed purpose, if I may say so.

Thank you, sir.

Bring that back to me and I'll finalize it after you pay the registration fee. You have money?

Right here.

Good. So upon those two steps being complete I can officially legitimize the vehicle and then for whatever reason a rickety, long-retired farm truck is back running on the public thoroughfare. Chicken feathers, cow dung, mouse droppings and all. You say you drove that thing?

Yes, sir. All around the place. It's a lot of fun.

I'll bet it is at that. But not on civic roads until you have a licence. Hear?

Yes, sir.

Now walk over to the clinic and get these papers marked. Then I'll find somebody to drive you back to Jimmy's place. Don't want to take a chance on the police interrupting this here business transaction, do you?

No.

Well then. Get going.

Robin loped the two blocks down and one over, which took him to the one-story cinder-block shelter that was the town's medical facility. Through the double glass door and inside the air-conditioned cool he bounded past the two empty waiting room chairs. The desk was unmanned so he was wordless down a familiar hallway, stepping briskly. Along the route he met a nurse coming out of the ladies room.

Oh. That was fast. You're here for his things?

Um. Not yet.

Oh. You just want to sit with him?

If that's okay.

You have time. I haven't called the funeral people yet.

I'll just be a few minutes.

Robin pushed open the door and did not look directly at the covered figure on the bed. The chair was where he had left it the previous evening. He sat down. For the sake of ceremony he doffed his hat and pulled out the document Teller had given him. He laid it upon the sheet near where he reckoned Jimmy's right hand reposed. He took the pen he'd been carrying and after a glance at the closed door made several Xs. He sat back and sighed, focused for the first time at the shroud where the face would be, fighting a shiver from the rushing air unit overhead. He silent-counted to sixty, then stood, folded the registration document and slid it into a pocket.

The nurse spoke as he passed her desk. I'm sorry we couldn't get word to you. Before he …

That's okay.

It happened fast after the last shot.

We were told that would most likely be how it went.

When I called he had just expired. About five minutes or less.

Thank you.

Will you pass the word to the family?

Yes.

She sighed and displayed a typewritten sheet. This is the list of people we have to contact. Guess I better get to it.

Okay.

Through the doors Robin stepped into the afternoon heat and strode away with a solid certainty that he would never again tread those halls.

On the way back he allowed himself a pause before the display window of the last womenswear shop in the town. It stood dark. He had passed it by a hundred times and often felt compelled to gaze at the forlorn, semi-clothed mannequin. The afternoon sun off the sidewalk gave her face a pale glow. Today the light even touched her saddened limbs and he saw that one arm was nearly coming away from the whole. An eerie significance in the assemblage struck him and hastened his continuation down the street. He knew, striding away, that this, too, was something he would not likely return to see.

Back in Teller's office he had to wait while a minor matter was settled with a farmer and then Teller excused himself to go to the washroom. Robin sat down and organized the paperwork on the desk so Teller would see it directly.

Well then. Teller re-sat and peered at the paper. Just Xs, eh? He's that far gone?

I'm not sure he was ever much for writing, sir. Not sure I ever saw a signature other than this X.

Neither can I, son, so this is just going to have to do. Let's get these stamped. Teller pulled a seal-making apparatus out of another drawer and opened a large ink pad. *Stamp.* Just so's we do get it done proper ... *stamp.* He wrote a signature. *Stamp.*

The phone on the desk rang. For a second it appeared Teller might ignore it. Then he laid a hand on the chiming instrument and put up a finger. He raised the receiver to an ear and leaned back in his chair. Yello … Yup. Yup. Uh-huh … What's that? Teller straightened and leaned over his desk as if studying the cracks and scars in the ancient oak. Do tell … Okay … Okay … Teller scribbled something on a pad of paper, frowning. Ah well. Right. Aha. What time was that now, exactly? Oh? You did, did you? Interesting. He did, did he? Okay. Right. No, no, I'm clearing up something now. I'll be by soon. Fine. Bye …

Teller's hang-up came with a hawk-eye glare of such concentration his target felt it might bore holes in his soul.

Now Robin.

Yes, sir.

Just what are you about here?

Getting Jimmy Scott's truck reg—

— Jimmy died an hour ago. You know that because they called you at the farm. Then you drove into town in Jimmy's new Ford. I saw you do it and asked about it and you said you had permission but that couldn't exactly be true, could it? Then you bring up all this business about the forty-two Chev and we start this here paperwork. Then you have the brazen temerity to go over to the clinic and sit with his mouldering body for two minutes while faking this little X-marking charade. If I didn't happen to be coroner of this district all these deceptions might have gone undetected. Teller nodded toward the phone. That was the clinic that called.

Jimmy wanted me to have it, sir.

Teller peered at the form on his desk. And now I see here that you've inserted your name as registered owner. He looked up and resumed his caustic glare. Did you buy this vehicle off Jimmy?

He wanted me to —

— have it. Yes I've heard that refrain sufficiently today thank you very much. Now whether it's true or not, here's official me almost transferring ownership of a motor vehicle to unlicensed minor you.

There's no law against it, sir. I checked.

You did, did you?

Only I can't drive it legal on the roads 'til I'm sixteen.

That would be accurate. And a thing to keep well in mind.

I plan to park it until then. Robin looked to the floor. I'll get my licence and come get it.

While arguments fly about whether or not you stole it from the rightful heir.

That would be my trouble, sir.

Never mind whose trouble it would be. You say Jimmy wanted you to have the truck. Did he actually leave a will?

I don't know.

I think you do.

I guess I do at that, sir. It's like you said. He didn't leave a will.

Well now ... Teller took off his glasses and sat back. Finally a little truth flowing here.

I'm sorry I misled you, sir.

Sorry isn't good enough.

No, sir.

Teller shifted and let the creaking springs of his chair fill the silence in the office. Well. This is quite the impasse then, isn't it?

I'll pay the fees right now.

It's not a matter of money ... Teller gazed out the window and then back at Robin. I ask you again, son. What are you about here?

Just doing what Jimmy said I could do, sir.

You've been away from home now how long? Two years?

A little over.

And you're how old exactly?

Just about sixteen, sir.

So fifteen.

Yes, sir.

And now Jimmy's dead. Are you going to head back home?

I thought I would.

You must.

I understand, sir.

You've got school, don't you? What grade are you going into?

Ten.

You've been catching the bus to the junior high in Gravelbourg?

Yes.

Well at least there's that, then. So you're heading back toward family.

Yes, sir. Out west.

You told me that. Do you need train fare?

I got cash. Jimmy paid me.

How come he paid you but not Sam?

He owed Sam a lot more.

How much do you have?

A hundred thirty-six dollars and some change.

Well now. Well now. Well now …

I'd be happy to pay whatever it takes if you'd just go ahead and register the vehicle, sir.

I didn't hear that.

I said I'd pay —

Quiet! Teller side-turned in his chair with a hand up. I'm trying to think here.

Sorry, sir.

No more of that … Teller swivelled to glare directly at Robin. You will learn, Master Robin Wallenco. You will learn and likely soon that sorry is a sad stand-in for remedy. Useless

in matters of business. Sorry is just a word and best left to the
bottom of the vocabulary barrel. In the case of man to man
… never used. For women … well … sometimes they need it.
But. Understand?

Uh-huh.

In the case of personal transgression you either fix it or hold
your piece. Got it?

Yes.

And speaking of understanding. Did I just hear you say that
after two years of farmhanding on that section Jimmy and his
family have been sitting on for generations you have the mere sum
total of around a hundred and thirty six dollars to show for it?

That's about right.

You're not a spendthrift are you, boy?

What does that mean, sir?

You don't go blowing your money on nothing and whooping good times or anything like that?

No. Saved most of it.

Well then. Pretty decrepit wages. Even considering room
and board.

I didn't need much.

Still. And Jimmy for certain didn't leave a will he didn't
tell me about?

Nope.

And nobody knows what he bequeaths to his heir and allots
to his creditors?

I'm not sure I understand.

His heir is his son.

Cullen.

Yes. Wherever he is and whenever he shows up. But you.
You are a creditor. He owes you. Or his estate does.

Jimmy took care of me.

Not relevant to this discussion.

Okay. Robin concentrated amid mental panic at not becoming lost inside the conversation. I think ... I think Jimmy might have meant for me to have the forty-two in place of wages, Mister Teller.

Oh really?

Yes.

He may well.

I think he did.

You do, do ya ... Well, heh. That makes sense when you consider. And you know ... Teller gestured a totality of the room in a wide arms-out motion and regarded Robin with a slow-smiling benevolence. Closing this place down is going to be a freedom experience, and yours might be near to the last bit of business this dying operation sees out. Hellfire, boy ... it might as well be for as odd a transaction as the registration of an antique vehicle to a desperado minor with indeterminate intentions. He shrugged and sank once again back into the creaky chair. I'm going to retire. Move to Arizona. If anyone ever asks a question ... Teller touched the registration paper with an index fingertip. Let some fellow in Assiniboia or Gravelbourg or even Regina deal with it. And besides. Why not?

Why not, sir?

Why not. Teller chuckled softly to himself. Have you read much, son?

I try. Every night if I've got a book.

Well a great writer once remarked of himself something like this: The point of going is not to find oneself but to get rid of oneself. Are you trying to get rid of yourself, young man?

I don't know.

Teller laughed. I think that's exactly the right answer. There's also this one that I like a lot. Teller gazed to the

ceiling and half closed his eyes. In the passion and heritage
of all elements of earthly presence and in our daily struggle
we might almost comprehend the meaning of our travail in
the context of human existence. And in your life you will do
things that make up a remembered biography. You will save a
life in both the corporeal and spiritual realm. Maybe rescue
a little old lady from a burning house. You will try to express
yourself to the greater world with little understanding of that
greater world. You will sit amid the murals of the great gal-
leries of the world and feel the psychic vibrations the artists
meant for you over the span of time and the chasm of mortality. You will travel madly across cities. Women will love and
despise you. Your family will misunderstand and adore you
while eschewing your works. You will find that time arrives
and departs inconsiderate and men scowl toward heavens as
if they existed.

Teller opened his eyes and levelled them at Robin. Jimmy
had scads of property. Worth near a hundred thousand, maybe
more. And you know there'll be so much equipment and parts
and odds and ends likely nobody will ever figure out what's
what and what's whose. Isn't that right?

More than likely.

And he took care of you like you were his own and you
worked for him as if he was your own. Right?

You could say that, sir.

And he most likely came to see as I do now that you're an
exceptional young man with untold stores of verve and acuity.
Among other things.

I'm not sure.

Well take it from me. From where I sit that's an accurate
observation.

If you say so, sir.

And this ancient pickup truck. Does anybody love it as much as you and Jimmy?

I dunno. Maybe.

Maybe. Do you know for sure? Does Cullen want the thing?

I don't know. When he was here last year he didn't even look at it.

Didn't even look at it, eh? Hmmm.

Mostly he drove the Ford. And argued with Jimmy.

Drove the Ford, did he?

Yup.

Well in that case. Fifteen dollars.

Sir?

The registration fee and insurance is fifteen dollars.

With a pounding heart Robin handed over the amount.

You sign here. Teller turned the paper over and indicated the place. Robin signed. Then Teller stamped and signed once more. Here's Jimmy's ... your copy. Keep it in the vehicle. He leaned to the side to rifle through a box on the floor. And the last bit. Brand new shiny licence plates.

Robin accepted the glinting metal panels with what he hoped were steady hands. Thank you, sir.

No further words necessary. Teller's smile showed curious signs of hurt. Now go.

I'll take the Ford.

Take the Ford and drive with fingers crossed. With any luck you'll get back to the farm without trouble. Otherwise I don't know anything about it. In fact I know little of anything that has happened today. In fact if anybody asks I can't remember and as far as I'm concerned nothing went on. Somebody I believed to be of legal age came in and had me process this vehicle registration.

Teller swept the papers on his desk into a bundle and dropped them into an open drawer.

And now I must go to the clinic and deal with the dead.

• • •

Cold tin plates in hand, Robin strode elated to the driveseat and exited town, steering with practised care, callused hands firmly on the wheel, feeling speed's freedom through the full-open windows. The newish Ford at forty miles per hour kicked up a rooster-tail of grime that dulled rearward vision nearly to nil. Ahead he spied a tail of flying grit. Decelerating and scanning the roadside for possible exits, he squinted farther at the oncoming speck. Sedan. Grey-brown surge cloud from out both sides. He pulled his hat low and held steady as their two dust clouds interwove and dissipated aside in the slow drift of an idle wind.

In ten minutes the great fields of his agrarian apprenticeship were in sight. On the last rise before the house the view gathered much of the whole quarter section, stretching vast away on all sides. One forty-acre dirt block of it was adorned with a distinct green anomaly. A rod-weeder malfunction — one foot of steel round end missing at a faulty weld — had caused enemy growth to pinstripe the fine brown-black soil. What other field in the Saskatchewan sprawl had such a jolly touch? Though reluctant to look at it, Robin could smile now. Jimmy had told him to, all along. But Jimmy's dead now. He frowned.

At the farm he eased the truck left into the yard and across to a shed. From the truck bed he gripped tires and carried them into the shop to fling onto the dirt floor. Dust rose and caught bright in the last sun of afternoon. The swirling grime settled back to allow the yellowing beams to bronze deeper the burnished rust patina of the 1942 Chevrolet half-ton pickup perched high upon four shop jacks.

He donned coveralls, flicked lights and compressor switch and began the yow yow air-wrench process of removing lug nuts. The shucked wheels formed a multi-circle pile where they were tossed, near the tire-mounting machine to one corner of the shed. Then with goggles, gloves, and gas bottle torch he bent to a bigger task. Shouldered in to the front wheel wells, he cut carefully. Molten nuggets fell from his work. Switching back and forth, eye measuring first and then gauging with ruler and calipers, he laboured for an elusive precision. Such was his concentration that a good while later he scarcely glimpsed a far doorway shadow. He killed the spewing flame.

Whatcha doin' there, young fella?

Robin put aside the torch-cutter and rose to see an oldster standing face-lit in shed light.

Hullo, Mister Carter.

It's late out, boy. Past dinnertime anyway.

Yes sir. Robin pulled the goggles away and over his head. I'm just getting to a bunch of work Jimmy set me to.

Jimmy's passed away.

Oh. You heard.

'Course I heard. Everybody's heard. Can't keep something like that a secret.

No sir.

Carter peered at Robin's equipment, squinting. What are you cutting?

Jimmy wanted the forty-two fixed.

And you're doing his bidding, is that right?

He didn't say not to … Robin paused to look up and meet Carter's eyes. … After he was gone. He hoped for a leavening of the hardness developing in the old man's voice. Jimmy knew he was going.

A dying man's last wish.

That's right.

Well. Pretty stupid if you ast me.

I'm just trying to keep busy, I guess.

Downright ridiculous.

May be. But I'm doing it.

Well. The old man scoff-spat and shoe-scuffed at the floor grit to come around and view the area of Robin's concentration. If that's what you have to do then machine working is just as good working as anything else I s'pose.

That's the way I figure it.

So what is it you're about here?

Cutting right now. Robin pointed. Going to widen out this area here.

Whatever for?

Put bigger tires on.

Why would you do a thing like that?

To get more speed at top end. For when you're on the highway. She's pretty high-geared.

Who's planning to drive this thing on any highway?

Oh I dunno. Just doing what Jimmy said.

Jimmy's passed away.

I know.

I still don't see what in hell you're machining for.

The tire clearance is different with these new ones on. Robin gestured toward the pile. If you crank it hard the tread rubs the frame. So I'm putting a notch where they go. And a bead just right where the tie rod ends will stop.

Let's have a look. The man went to a two-hand-on-knee crouch close so Robin could smell his leftover hand-roll tobacco breath. You're up to what down here?

Cleared over this way. Robin pointed. Then going to build up this area here.

Better put it slightly up over there. Carter pointed. Otherwise you're gonna have this problem here. See? Carter knocked an ossified knuckle against the frame.

Gee. Is that right?

Git in there and crank it.

Robin clambered to lean into the driver's side and yanked the steering wheel.

Hear that? It's clankin'.

How do I fix it?

Well it's pretty clear you gotta clean off this here edge with the grinder. Then lay the same size bead over here. That there'll give you the governing part for the rods. You gotta keep this part here clear ...

Thanks, Mister Carter.

The protection goggles went back onto Robin's face and with torch in hand he assumed a careful stance.

The old man straightened and looked around. When's Cullen gonna come?

Not sure exactly. I called the camp. He's in the field. They said they'd get word to him.

Huh. Shame he wasn't here.

Well last we heard he said he'd come down as fast as he could.

His dad layin' there all dyin'.

Nobody knew how long Jimmy could go. I saw him last night. Seemed okay enough.

Well they were never close as a father and son might generally want to be.

Jimmy told me that.

And that boy never was much attached to the place.

I guess that's why he went out to the oil works.

Yep. Pitiful. Carter wandered a few steps and kicked a machine. Something like this might nevera happened.

What? Robin raised his goggles. You mean the rod weeder?

Damn right I mean the rod weeder.

Jimmy said it wasn't my fault.

Don't matter about that now. Jimmy's passed away. But Cullen'll want to sell the machinery.

If he doesn't intend to stay on on the place.

Oh he'll sell all this here stuff. Then lease the land out. That's what he said to me when he left last time. Said I'm not coming back unless and until the old man is passed away or selling out and I'm just here to clean up the mess.

Aw I don't think Cul really feels all that bad about it.

No matter. Carter pointed to the broken section of the idle rod weeder. You better keep that torch hot and reattach this here piece that's missing.

Jimmy said a weld most likely wouldn't work. That's what the problem was in the first place. It'd just knock off again. Needs the whole one sidebar section replaced or something like that. He thought he'd wait 'til next year to go buy it.

Whether it holds or not. It's improper to put away equipment for winter with parts damaged or missing. I know people around here do it all the time but it's not proper.

Well I suppose I could.

You got the piece?

Sitting over there on the bench.

Here I'll give you a hand.

As outside dark developed on the shop walls they formed two-figure shadows from the lamp and hanging bulb. With combined coordination of three hands and one torch they attended to the metal repair.

There now. Looks good.

Yes it does. It's better this way. You were right.

'Course I'm right. Why wouldn't I be? Been farming this dirt under us for close on fifty years.

Always the same place?

Right up there over the rise. You seen it.

Yes.

Don't need anything more than a piece of land and a tractor.

Well.

What're you still doing here anyway, boy? By now you should be on a bus back where you came from.

Jimmy needed me.

I'm talking about right now. Don't you have family?

Yes. I'm going back there. Fast as I can.

Well you do that.

I will.

Cleared out of the house yet?

Got just about everything packed. Going to spend a last night here and get going.

Got travel money?

Yup, I'll hitch a ride to Kincaid … Robin spoke without looking at the old man. Get the bus to Swift Current. Then train it from there.

Just shut the doors and windows. I'll see after the place 'til Cullen comes. Likely he'll want to contract the harvest. Either way I'll give him a hand.

Jimmy said you'd see to all that.

Yep.

Good to know, sir.

It is, isn't it. Carter leaned cross-legged against a wall and pulled cigarette makings from a pocket. Well I hope you learned something. Working here. Staying with Jimmy.

I did. I hope I did. I sure am grateful to him.

As you should be.

Carter lit his smoke and strolled toward the door. He stopped to kick at more equipment and looked sourly back at Robin, then wandered into the darkness.

Now alone, Robin worked quickly. After an hour he stowed the welding gear and lowered the '42 down to stand upon four wheels. He hefted its old battery out and by flashlight outside performed switchery on the Ford. He installed the newer power cell into the '42, then wiped hands and tested the old truck's starter. With his fingers he gauged the brushes, the rotor, the generator.

As a last important factor in the plan he pulled from the junk pile a hand-pump fuel tank he'd repaired some time ago. It fit snug in the bed just behind the cab and he fastened the pre-rigged stays of it by heavy bolts to keep it from rolling. Then a restart of the truck and a swing around just past the reach of the shed lights aside the big fuel reservoir to fill gas and then the reserve tank up so full there was no slosh. He over-severely tightened down the plug and knuckle-tapped the thing double for reassurance.

Then the all-important travel checklist: tools, rope, clamps, tackle, motor oil, light bulbs, signal bulbs, fuses, jerry can, spark plugs ... And the big etcetera of his clothes and bedroll. Water in two plastic gallon jugs, packed under the seat or at the foot of the passenger side or on the seat beside him or in the box as necessary. When all was secured he patted the '42's fender and strode up to the house.

Washing at the sink he shook water from hands and for only a reflective moment regarded the wet depths of his mirrored face.

A supper of banana peanut butter sandwiches with the last of the bread. He managed a bath without dozing and did the proper things to ready for sleep. More fatigued than he realized, he stumbled to the front door to thumb down the master lightswitch.

Underwear-clad he lay stretched upon the couch where the largest house window overlooked descending territory north and away in blackness.

He sat momentarily in the silence, gazing to distant pins of light, then turned to flick on the cabinet stereo with the only record he cared to listen to.

With closed eyes, imagining, he let the Beach Boys lure him to sleep with images of a little surfer girl …

• • •

Dawn lanced him through the wide window. Robin stretched with eyes still closed and rolled to another side. Further slumber took the next ten minutes.

When light was fuller about the landscape he rolled from sleep and washed face and hands and rinsed mouth. He gathered food from the fridge. Lunchmeat and cheese placed in a crude cooling foil pack meant for beer. Without sentiment he strode the yard and swung open the driver's door. It felt right to run a hand over the cracked leather and slide behind the wheel. In the instant before starting he took what he knew would be a last gaze out to where he'd pulled down an old barn, oiled machinery, shovelled rotten grain into a growling auger. He'd waited in sweaty truck interiors with windows closed to fend grit and particulated barley beards, choosing swelter over dust. Though cautious, he'd never completely avoided the itch-scratch frenzy as micro-husk needles cut his skin, waiting until Saturday for a full-on bathe to clean the farming off his body.

He did not look back at the farm as he left it though there was a twinge in his heart knowing he might never again see the place. Gearing the '42 up to speed down the road exhilarated him, wiping the sentiment away. The air of early day bit slightly as it should, coming in a side vent rush. He drove quick first north then west on a road devoid of traffic.

After half an hour a lonely church that meant something to him presented itself on a ridge in the mile distance. He turned off and rolled up the rutted path into the yard. Around the far side he knew was sufficient space to situate out of sight from passing traffic.

As he moved to tuck the truck behind he was jolted to find a big-finned Cadillac convertible idling in the long shadow of the steeple. An unconscious man slumped at the driver's seat. Robin could hear snoring once the '42 was shut off even though the perfect purr of the Caddy's flowing exhaust was audible too. He stepped to the ground not knowing if he should disturb the sleeper by closing the door.

Before Robin could contemplate further the man started, snorting. Hey … He looked about him and shifted to regard the antique truck and teenage boy observing him. Where'd you come from?

I'm parked here. For a minute.

Huh … Well. He stared at the truck and at Robin. I guess that's okay. The man switched off the Cadillac's ignition and with an audible pull of the door handle lurched from the vehicle. He wore a rumpled pair of dress pants and untucked shirt. What time might it be?

I dunno. Seven maybe.

Yeah. That makes sense. He stretched and blinked blearily toward the weathered prairie chapel. Some place, huh?

What? The church?

Yeah. Stuck like a big wooden knob in the middle of this here wheat field. Nobody around. Unlikely place. Kinda reaffirms faith doesn't it? In some weird way? Or supposed to …

Not sure. I guess.

You wanna go in there?

Um. I hadn't thought of it.

You can just walk in. Catholics trust the world. The man progressed to the front and up the stairs. Here. You see? He two-hand-yanked the arched entry open.

Robin left the truck door hang in anticipation of a quick exit from a situation that had him quizzical nearly to the point of forgetting why he was there. When he remembered he decided to forget the man at least temporarily and stepped along the side of the church toward the graveyard. It was a walk of fifty yards or so and he gazed pointedly toward the place he knew he knew and had known for the time he'd occupied the flat lands.

For five minutes Robin stood and then stooped aside the grave marked "Appalonia." He stared at the carved stone and the mossy covering and tried to make his mind photographic, running a finger through the etched letters and across the dates below.

He sidled back to the church and saw that the man stood semi-visible in the dark maw of the half-opened narthex. C'mon up, boy.

I dunno.

Suit yourself. But by the way. He pointed to the nearby rise where the road disappeared over the brow. There's cops just over there down the way.

There is?

Better come talk to me. There's a way around.

Once inside Robin near shuddered in the country morning cold silence of the place.

The man slumped into a pew.

Robin approached. Are you from around here?

The man made to answer but then did not speak. Robin could hear his breathing.

Huh. A bemused lazy regard through half-open lids. What a question.

I just wondered if you knew the landscape hereabouts. I need pointing. I have to get off this road.

An eyebrow raise and shifting of posture. You don't say.

How do I keep going west without using Forty-Three?

Well. If you don't want to be seen you shouldn't be on it in the first place.

I figured anytime before seven or so.

You figure probably right. Later on they'll be checking for purple gas. But not right now. Right now it's not your gas they'll be looking to.

How's that?

Me. I'm your heatbag, kiddo. The Mounties are looking for me.

Oh.

The man sat straight, resting his forearms on the pew back. Be careful who you marry, kid.

Okay.

And whatever you do never drink with people you don't know.

Okay.

Ever had a drink?

Beer. With supper once or twice.

Yeah well. I'm talking about something else.

Okay.

But anyway. What can I do for you, my young friend? Direct you somewhere?

I'm not sure.

Is that vintage farm vehicle you're in properly licensed?

Yes.

And are you?

Not exactly.

Not at all would be more like it, eh?

Yes.

Well then stay off the main roads.

I plan to. Much as possible.

Though that's a rough go too. You meet a cop on one of those farm spurs and he'll look you over good. Halt you to check gas colour for sure.

I made sure it was blue.

How? Ink?

Bought up some before I left. Got the can under the seat. Put in just enough to sort of scrub the purple.

Smart. But don't let 'em find that jerry can you're sitting on.

Got it stowed away pretty good.

I saw it easy enough.

Well I'll cover it up more. And I got money to refill it.

And you have what's in that forty-gallon bed tank there.

Yeah.

What colour's it?

It's farm gas.

Well. They'll think you're heading out to refuel a tractor or something if you can convince them you're from around wherever it is they stop you near. You might avoid them thinking you're a thief even before they get to understanding you're underage and certainly not the registered owner of that antique.

I got papers that say I am.

And all of some-teen years old.

I'll be sixteen soon.

Ha ha … The man sat back. He took a slim bottle from a pants pocket and swigged. Where are you going, if I might ask?

BC.

Ho! And where you come from?

South of Glenbain.

Whoa, twenty some miles away already. But you've got far to go.

I just started.

I'll say. And where might you be going once you get to British Columbia?

Not too sure. Out Long Beach way.

Where's that?

Across Vancouver Island and out on the west edge.

Ho! You're not from around here?

Originally from Qualicum Beach.

I think I was there once. Oysters. You can walk out on the beach and dig up a whole dinner in ten minutes.

That's the place.

Fresh sea breeze all the time. Nice weather even in winter.

Uh-huh.

But there's things to be said for out here on the flat land.

I agree.

It wasn't always so. There's been hard times out on this territory. Even harder than now. Way worse.

I've heard the stories, sir.

An impetuous glance upward through the nave and to the high-mounted altar Jesus. No lack of ambition in this one, Lord. Another swig, chuckling. He corked the flask and slid it back into a pocket. Is this a spur-of-the-moment thing or are you determined?

I been planning.

I suppose you have. The man regarded Robin gravely and head-gestured outside. But there's peril every step, eh?

Guess you could call it that.

Well. We're fine here for a bit yet. They only set up about a half hour ago.

How do you know?

Saw them from a way off. Before I pulled in here to catch a nap. They knew I was coming this way so I knew to watch out for them.

Oh.

But I'm a goner anyway. Plan to give myself up.

For real?

Yup. No sense dragging this out. I just wanted to sit down for a minute or two. Have a drink. Get a moment in this chapel. My people are buried out back.

Mine too.

There's relatives of somebody behind every church in the territory, my friend.

I know. I guess that means you are from around here.

Once was. Only my dead kin are still in residence now. Mother is just out that window there by the seventh station of the cross. Nobody knows where my dad might be but I have uncles and aunts and cousins out there galore. Dead of just about everything. Age. Disease. Accidents too. Some of them younger than me.

I heard things like that.

Mostly unsafe working conditions.

My grandmother is out there. She died of cancer. My boss's brother got killed in a tractor rollover.

Lots of those. Machinery accidents. Weather mishaps. There was a tornado whipped through here last spring. Sent water tanks flinging into granaries like Matchbox toys. The man paused and tapped his chest to let out a resonant burp. You can freeze to death eight months of the year for crying out loud. And dead children too. And mothers in delivery. And

kids with whooping cough and fevers and poxes. Etcetera. They
didn't have doctors all the time.

Gee.

You can die of heartbreak too.

I suppose.

Forgive me, kid. That's a deeper subject than the present
discussion warrants.

If you say so.

The man lay back down and riffled in his clothes as if having forgotten where he'd located the liquor. Don't listen too
much to what I prattle on about. He took a healthy pull from
the half-full mickey. I am after all at least slightly drunk. But
I will tell you this one. Why my father isn't out there in the
ground. He was a bastard, that's what. One day drunk he came
down the stairs with his gun. The target-shooting one. He
pointed it at my mother and me as we sat on the living room
couch. Mom told him to put it down but he just kept waving it
at us from one to the other and laughing. Then he fired. Either
accidentally or on purpose we never knew for sure. It passed
closer to me than Mom. The hole in the window behind us
was still there when I drove past the house a few years ago. It
isn't a big hole. The gun was a twenty-two. But there it was.
Years later.

He took another drink, sighing.

Robin tried not to watch the prone orator's lusty swallowing
make an odious laryngeal fluctuation in his throat. The sight
repelled him. The sound of the man's voice and the words he
was saying, too, made him as uneasy as he could imagine being.
He reflexed a step backward before he could resist doing it. Is
there anything I can do for you, mister?

Ha ha ha. Did you believe that, kid? The story?

I don't know. Why wouldn't I?

Aw, man. What does it matter?

I don't know.

All it means is bones in the ground and the names. Katerina. Maria. Fatima. Etcetera. He waved the mickey-bottle in a sweeping gesture. Get it, kid?

I'm sorry. Are you feeling okay? Should I go get help?

Naw, kid. Sorry to talk like that. A bit scrambled I know. Katerina is my grandmother by the way. And listen. She laboured alongside grandfather. To dig the rancid granaries clean. Careful not to step too close to the auger for danger of losing a foot to the winding blade. It was real work in those days, kid. And you'll notice not many of them that lie out there got past seventy. Some not even sixty.

Yes, sir.

And me likely not even forty.

I wouldn't know about that, sir.

Just live clean is all I'd have you do for me. Or for the world. Mostly for yourself.

I'll try.

But for now. The man stood with such abrupt lurching purpose Robin near flinched and did actually rear slightly back again to lean with one hand on a pew corner and look down and then up again for the man's next move. We have to see what can be done about your continued western travel.

I'd sure appreciate the help.

Come with me, young lad.

They walked along the pews to a door at the side that stuck somewhat and had to be shouldered to reveal the narrow stairs to the balcony. From there was a ladder up which the man bounded with surprising speed. He shouldered open the trap-door above. Robin watched from the floor.

Come on, boy.

Is there room up there?

Just enough. We'll survey from here.

Up through the belfry floor Robin poked head and one shoulder. He climbed alongside the man in the tiny space so each could observe the surrounding landscape through one facet of the lantern gaps.

We could climb out and try to get up the spire. Always wanted to do that.

Not me, sir.

Ha ha. Just kidding. We can see fine from here.

I see the cops.

They're still there, all right. Not for much longer though.

How long do you think?

Well pretty soon they'll be figuring they missed me. Five or ten more minutes. Then they'll plan out their next move. Only two men and one car. That'll limit their options. Considering that this here church is the only structure for a good five miles around you have to think they'll check it before they go any-place else.

I've got to get out of here then.

Yes you do. But listen to my plan now. The man pointed up the church drive and past a fence toward a rise. See that farm rut over there? The one with the big mound of dirt by it?

Yeah.

That goes for a good piece up toward that group of silos and beyond.

I see it.

Okay. I'm gonna ring these bells.

What?

There hasn't been regular service in this parish since the diocese lost their last priest. And that was a while back. And it's a Wednesday, no?

I think it's Thursday.

There you go. Even on a Sunday morning those Mounties would be surprised to hear these bells start up over here.

I don't get you.

Kid lookit. I'm working out a diversion for you, eh? You slip back down to that jalopy of yours and wait for the noise to start. Then motor quiet as you can up the approach there and pause the other side of that dirt pile. Soon as they hear bells the cops'll strike their pose out there and speed up the road and turn in here to investigate. Soon as they're moving I'll see it and stop the carillon show. That's your signal to move. If we time it right you'll be out of their sight long enough for you to get up that rise past the silos and over to the next farm. They're not looking for a teenage runaway in a museum pickup anyway so you got that counting for you.

I'm not a runaway.

We're all running away, kid. But that doesn't matter. Now listen. You can keep going on there past the mound and beyond. It's rough in some bits but just keep moving straight. It's a good long way by my recollection. Comes out somewhere on Number Four.

Okay but. What does carol on mean?

A cacophony of bells.

Oh.

And don't ask me what cacophony means.

Okay. So bells?

Yes bells. Although the term might more literally refer to something like a chime I guess but who's splitting hairs?

Nobody I guess.

Do me a personal favour kid and stay in school. Get an education. It'll handle a lot of stuff for you.

I'll see about it.

Make sure you do.

You really want to give yourself up?

Yeah. There's no good even talking about it.

If you say so.

So get going. The cops'll be moving soon so you gotta go. We don't have much time to put this master deviation into place.

I sure do thank you.

Don't mention it.

What's your name, by the way?

Doesn't matter.

I'd feel better knowing.

In another life kid we would have the fun and the honour of being pals maybe. But.

The man held a handshake hand out. Robin took it.

Name's Ben.

Ben. I'm Robin.

Nice to have met you Robin. Now fly like one. Go.

On the descent he chanced just one glance upward and got to see the flask out. Ben did not look at him but gulped deep and faced out to the prairie in the direction of the agreed plan.

The peal began before he could hit the starter and as the heretofore-comforting silence vanished inside the ardent tintinnabulation the vibration made him strangely know that others existed on this freshening morning. With moistening palms Robin tooled out of the churchyard and sped up to the appointed hiding place where even over the rumble of the '42's idle he could clearly hear the steeple serenade and even spy a flash or two of Ben's face through the belfry vents as he yanked down upon the bell cable.

Then quiet.

Robin eased back into gear and rolled from the shadow of the dirt and opted to just drive straight ahead without looking back and continued away along the edge of the open field where earthen tracks told of many trucks before him. For a measure of authenticity he made sure to rest his tan elbow out the window. With its rolled work shirt, an emblem of the universal working farmer.

Once behind the silos he swerved off the track into the deep shadow of the granaries and paused a little, then manoeuvred through a crack in a tumbleweed-clogged fence so he could peer at the church. Sure enough there stood a cherry-topped sedan by the steps and seconds later the expected three figures — cuffed prisoner flanked by two uniforms — emerged from the darkened door and down steps to the police car. He watched Ben's insertion into the backseat. The police moved firm and careful. They did not look around the churchyard or in any distant direction.

• • •

A couple of hours down the slow road he stopped between a near-collapsed shed and a jumble of abandoned machinery to pull out a sandwich. There had been no vehicle following or ahead, and aside from a far-off tractor weeding summer fallow there was nothing to see that moved. From where he munched, perched on a rusted harrow frame, there was faint view of the empty road. He breathed a long withheld breath at having convincingly avoided the Royal Canadian Mounted Police. He ate quickly.

Back underway he knew by memory of the map Jimmy Scott had mounted on the kitchen wall that the field edge trails he'd been following would eventually end at a main road. Number Four, as Ben had said. The question then would be north or south? Or keep going west over whatever rut, open field, ditch draw, cut, or whatever else might be in his way until out of flatland country. For now he saw amid the general blue the far wisp of an approaching storm head.

A lineup of silver-sided homestead dwellings showed along the horizon and he made for them across raw land and was glad to find a shed big and open enough to park within. Just in time. Water hammered down in the noon-day dusk, the fork flashes close by. Robin snoozed in the cab. He lay against the kitbag with feet out the window and through occasional awakenings noted drips and drops from the shed's perforated roof.

Afterward the wet-scent air balmed both driver and engine on the steady trek over muddied ruts. He steered on the grassy centre and overgrown sides whenever possible. Through crests and gullies and around fence gaps when they occurred and through when they did not. When obstacled by gates or remnants of, Robin used cutters he'd brought along to allow passage and binder wire and pliers to make repairs.

He hit the main road at mid-afternoon and opted a southern leg just long enough to locate a likely field trail due west again. He made progress shooting along long hay stands on either side of the road, near high enough to conceal him from a level observer. After an hour or so he emerged from a deep break on a track he'd lost at one point and only barely found after fording a semi-dry stream to take the sole route to the other lip without falling sideways off the incline.

Just as the geography flattened out a man stood before him on the trail. Robin spied a stopped tractor in a near field with swather attached. He slow-wheeled up to the man and stopped but did not pull the truck out of gear.

You got the parts? The man spoke into his window.

Uh …

The hose? He peered into the '42's bed. Where's it at? And the bushings and stuff. Been three hours now.

I'm not the —

Chuck sent you out, didn't he? I told him to. Gall-darn if he didn't.

No. I didn't get sent by Chuck.

Then what are you? Trespassing?

Um. I suppose so.

Oh come off it. You're kidding, right? Where's the hose? We gotta fix the hydraulics on that thing before it gets dark.

Robin opted then to shut down and step to the dusty earth. I'm kinda lost. He leaned against his door as casually as he could. Not from around here.

Didn't think I knew you.

Actually all I need is a pointer. Does this route come out anywhere near a town or anything?

Wait a minute here. You're not carrying the parts I need to fix that there swather?

No.

You didn't get sent here by Chuck Hazely who I sent back into Cadillac to get a pressure hose and attachments like about half a day ago?

Nope.

Dang. Musta had to go all the way over to Shaunavon. Well.

Though used to the man's type Robin was at least slightly discomfited at a close lookover of himself and the truck.

You got tools in there?

Some.

Socket set?

Yeah.

The one Chuck left me is busted. And I need a needlenose and a bunch of screws.

Well I'll see what sizes I've got.

Robin made for the tool box.

Out on the prairie the machinery stood idle. Anyone who'd ever worked land as these two had knew they had to work fast as the afternoon was aging and the weather might change. Robin broke open his tools and the man wandered a hand through the implements.

I think you got what we need. At least to get the job started.

Okay.

If you want to grab that there shank I'll wrench the drawbar off this bastard.

Is it seized?

Gall-darn hydraulics gave up on this last section of clamps. Totally screws up the bearing hanger. Hold fast on that torsion bolt there. I'll give 'er a turn.

An hour of screw-turning and ratchet-wracking ensued and neither were fully aware of a truck pulling up to swerve to a dusty halt beside their complicated works.

Hey, fellers.

Damn, Chuck. Where'd you go? Regina and back?

Nearly. They didn't have the right boot and washer assembly at the first place. Second neither. Had to scoot all the way to Swift Current. Then wait while they plumbed around their parts department looking for this and that.

Well. We nearly got it all apart here.

I see that. Chuck swung a cardboard box loosely rattling of metal and hard plastic. He glanced at Robin. Who do we have here?

My name's Robin Wallenco, sir.

Young fella stopped by to help. Says he was trespassing.

Ha! That cute old Chev your transportation?

It is.

Drove one myself some decades back.

Well. This one's still running.

Oh hell, son, you keep oil in the crank and air in the tires you can't kill these old motors. Question is why drive a unit that's barely got a heater for the winter. Boils over in summer. And can't hardly make over forty-five-miles-an-hour out on the highway?

I like this truck, sir. It's the first vehicle I ever drove.

Heh heh. Reason enough I suppose.

He lent me a good hand with this foul-up, Chuck. And now if you're finished jawing here you might maybe give us both help to install this mount hardware.

You sticking around to see us through this, boy?

Um. Well I kind of wanted to keep on as far as I could go before dark. I was heading west.

On this rut? It pretty well stops at a washout five or so miles down the way there. Why not take the main road?

Um.

Though each had work-ready wrenches and/or screwdrivers in hand the three paused looking at each other over the awkward conversational gap. Then a gleam of understanding brightened Chuck's eyes.

How old are you, Robin?

Not old enough to drive legally on the roads, sir.

Hold back on that sir business. Name's Chuck Hazely. This fella's name is Norm if he hasn't already told you. This here's my field. That other one too. And all the ones around here.

Pleased to meet you, Chuck.

You want to stay for the time it takes to get Norm here going back at this swath job? We'll take you along and give you supper and a bed if you care to.

Well.

And we'll point you along a better direction to head west. Or any which way.

As in typical field repair, progress was punctuated with dropped tools, misplacements, stubbed fingers, and general cursing. But there were three sets of hands. Missing or broken parts were haywire-rigged back to existence and operation. Before quitting time Robin and Chuck stood back as Norm fired up the tractor and actioned the stalk-cutting blades through the amber grain and conjured a dust demon behind in the roiling late afternoon breeze.

At workday's end the two trucks wound down through a farther cut similar to the one Robin had negotiated earlier and proceeded southwest along the dry creek until onto a well maintained farm road. A collection of barns and Quonset sheds appeared above the wheat horizon. Robin calculated that by the time they arrived at where he presumed the residence was they would be looking-distance from the main route he'd been avoiding. He surveyed the layout for likely escape routes. Norm waved him to a parking spot near what looked like a bunkhouse.

Chuck stood watching him approach the main house. My. I didn't ask it before but that is a forty-one model, isn't it?

Forty-two.

A rare one.

So I'm told.

Well, like I said. Times past we all drove these beauties. What are your plans? Takin' her to a place for restoration?

I'm just trying to get out west.

West. How far?

Far as you can go without driving into saltwater.

Oho. That's far.

Well. I know more or less where I'm going when I get there.

Good to know you're not gonna get lost. Anyhoo. You can go with Norm over to the bunkhouse and clean up if you like. Supper's in the house when you get through with that.

Thanks.

Thank you. You and your tools saved us a couple of hours out there.

Glad to do it.

Supper was full-spectrum farm fodder. Mrs. Hazely was a woman of British background and produced in quantity the most savoury-glorious fluffy Yorkshire puddings Robin had ever seen. Amid the knobs of gravy-covered baked goods lay great hunks of semi-rare beef and mounded potato. With stacked carrot rails and caramelized Brussels sprouts the general eating was intense and intent.

Norm forked back the last of his meat portion and leaned away. Well Robin you are a captive now, eh? You've gotten into Maeve's cooking and next you'll be looking to get yourself a steady job on this here Hazely spread.

Robin would have responded but for the fullness of meat and potatoes in his mouth. Chuck piped: He's a shoo-in if he can stand living in that outhouse I mean bunkhouse with you as his sole roommate.

Oh there there boss. Norm smirked confidently. I'm not so bad.

We'll see by the way this guy either lingers around tomorrow morning looking for something to do or kicking gravel out the driveway with that fine pickup.

Well we'll see.

I suppose.

Yessir I reckon.

Time will tell.

It'll all come out in the wash.

Tomorrow's another day.

Proof'll be in the pudding.

Never can say for sure.

Slim pickins.

He's an actor in the movies.

Will you gentlemen please quit! Maeve did not speak in a raised voice. Her authority needed no amplification in the cathedral of her dining room. The patter immediately fell tacit. Robin will do as he wishes to do. Won't you, my dear?

I will, yes. Thank you, ma'am.

And I thank you young boy for bringing these hands in off the field in time for supper. A meal that depends on timing, appreciation, and responsibility. She smiled. Qualities I detect are latent aspects of your still-forming character.

Mrs. Hazely I'm grateful you think I'm okay. I sure like your food.

Thank you, Robin.

And no matter what it's like in the bunkhouse. After a meal like this I'll be interested to see what breakfast looks like around here.

Laughter.

In the bunkhouse Norm pulled a near-full bottle of rye from a dresser drawer and proffered it to Robin.

You partake?

Nope. Thanks.

Ever drank?

Jimmy. That's the man I used to work for. Gave me half-a-beer with supper the odd time.

Heh. Norm poured an inch of whisky in a glass and topped the drink with water. Chuck doesn't 'specially like it but I keep a bottle around.

You're the second guy I've run into today that likes his liquor.

Oho. Who you been hanging with?

Not even sure. I like to think he's okay now but I happen to know the cops got him. No idea why.

Norm's dark-faced look took Robin by surprise. The drink hung suspended in his hand momentarily. Then Norm relaxed and took a gulp.

Well. *Glug.* Sure glad we're safe here in the bunkhouse and away from any who would interfere with us. Man ought to be able to take a drinka liquor without bother from anybody.

I guess. Do you mind if I sack out now? I'm kinda tired.

Go right ahead. Another shot of this stuff and I'll be fading out pretty soon myself.

Robin shucked off clothes, slumped onto the bunk he'd been shown to, and faced the wall.

• • •

Light accompanied the rustle of clothing and the sense that something was moving in close proximity. Then a hand to his shoulder. Opened eyes showed him that Norm was pulling on his clothes and peering out the window. Robin lurched upright.

Whoa boy. No need to jump.

What's going on?

Any reason you'd know why the Mounties are here?

What!

You got a sensitivity to them?

Robin glanced out the bunkhouse portal and was glad the old glass was roiled and tinted and the opening small. The patrol car parked by the house was impossible to miss even through the distortion.

Why are they here?

Well if you don't know then all we can do is speculate. Might be checking for purple gas. Might be looking into some tractor thefts down the road. Who knows.

I'd kind of like to avoid them.

Me too if you want to know the god's honest truth. We could sneak out and let Chuck handle things.

I'd hate to just leave and not thank Mister and Missus Hazely.

Don't you worry about that. I'll take care of your respects and good manners when I get the next chance. But for now we gotta get out of here.

Robin pulled on jeans and shirt. Are they in the house?

Just walked in. We got a minute or two.

They might not hear the truck at first but we'd have to drive by the house.

Not the way we're going.

If you say so.

Transfer of belongings went quick and both were in the cab inside sixty seconds. Parked as it was on a slight incline Robin had only to ease off the brake to let the '42 creep silently from any in the house who might see.

Just ease her down that rut by the fuel tanks and coast right into the cut you can't see right now but'll be right in front of us just past the shed there.

Robin steered as instructed down steepening dust tracks so that less than a minute later he could jump the truck alive as they barrelled toward a muddy creekbed. He revved the cold engine and fought the jerky steering wheel.

Turn down the stream. We gotta get off this road. Can she take it?

I don't know. Does it get any rougher?

Just about like this all the way. Stay on the banks if you can. Mud's not that deep.

It was a skidwheel sideslip motorized sluice of a drive.

After most of a bumpy mile with no delays Norm was impressed. You're doing great, boy. Now look for a ford on the right. Might just be a stick stuck in the bank.

Is that it?

Yeah. You can see the track there, can you?

Faint.

Well it'll be the only notice you get.

Robin lurched the truck onto a low part of the bank but nonetheless had to spin the back wheels in a rising gout of semi-dry mud, rocks, and twigs. Moments were that it seemed they would recede back into the dirty stream. Finally they gripped onto stern ground leading skyward through shrub land.

When you get to the open you keep us going until the road. There's a granary there you hide us behind. I'll climb up and see if the coast is clear.

They neared a driveway that Robin surmised was a route up to the Hazely farmhouse. He duly pulled behind the building that was there. Norm slinked from the truck wordless and without closing the door gripped onto the stationary ladder up the granary side and climbed from sight. Seconds later he was back down.

Hightail it, kid!

Robin did, though to minimize detection he took it easy for the first mile down the grassy centre and shoulder of the easy slope until the rooster tail of dust they put up would be lost under the roll of the land visible from the Hazely settlement.

You're smart. Drive on the scrub. Keep the dust down for a bit. That is smart.

Thanks.

You know how to run from the cops. Good for you.

Thanks. But ...

I done this lotsa times. You?

Just started.

Well. You can tell me all about it over eggs and coffee. Especially coffee.

Traffic on the road was light and of little concern even
when the secondary they ran on for a half hour ended at the
major Number Thirteen east-west artery. Norm guided Robin
to a nestled diner on the broad main thoroughfare running
by the quiet businesses of downtown Eastend. They parked at
back and settled into a cracked-Naugahyde booth just as two
other farmers were leaving. The place was noise-crowded and
in a cigarette smoke dim that when combined with the frying
bacon wood-scent nearly camouflaged the coffee steam aroma
rising from their cups.

Everyone greeted Norm by name.

Kid, sorry I skedaddled you out of there before you could
tuck into one of Maeve's famous breakfasts.

That's okay. I'm just glad we got away from the cops.

What's your issue? Trying to get out of school?

The other way around. I want to get to school.

And home?

That's mostly right.

Well. No man can argue with that. Going home's a power-
ful instinct. I spent a good bit of my younger life doing nothing
but wanting to go home. It tears at you, doesn't it?

It kinda does.

Well we don't really have to talk about it. Mostly let's eat
this fine breakfast here. Did I mention I'm buying?

Thanks, Norm.

The hunger of men on the run set in as heaps of grease-
fried potato and scrambled eggs disappeared from their plates.
Coffee continued flowing as toast-wrapped bacon got gobbled
down in gnashing bites. Norm sat back.

Guess how old I am, kid.

I dunno. Not too old.

Old enough to have fought in the war.

Oh.

Italy. You heard of the First Special Service Brigade?

No.

Well. It was an elite unit. Sharp. They recruited me because I'm Cree. Can you tell?

Norm turned his profile for Robin to examine.

I guess. Don't know if I know too many Indians.

Well take a good look. And these hands.

A quick movement and two talons ground into Robin's forearms. He dropped the fork he'd been aiming at the last of the hashbrowns, getting a sense of what it might be like to be clapped in irons.

As quick as he'd gripped Robin's arms Norm released them. Learned tracking from my uncle when I was young. Still had the skills when the army come calling.

Did you fight?

Did I fight! Ha. Did I do anything but fight is the question. Darn little. Aside from marching and polishing boots at first. The training was boring awful. But then it got kind of interesting. All sorts of fierce things to do to a guy and especially how to kill fast and quiet. We were the hard edge in every move they made. The high command. They sent us in under dark. Under barrage. Under camouflage. Everything. I got damn good at it.

At fighting.

Yep. Actually kind of too good at it. Habitual, you might say. We were stopping Hitler, after all. Violence was the way. Norm took a long drink of coffee and rolled his eyes to the ceiling. That's kinda why I need to steer wide of the Mounties, generally.

Violence?

I been in some fights. I avoid the cops.

That's what I'm going to do until I'm old enough to drive.

You seem old enough for a lot of things.

I try.

Not much else a fellow can do.

That's the way I figure it.

Well my friend, I can tell you for sure that I'm wise enough to know not to ask a man — or a boy — too many questions about why he's doing whatever he seems to need doing. Including running from the law.

I appreciate that.

And into the bargain I'm an expert at leaving town. All sorts of ways of doin' it. I'll show you how to get out of here.

Great.

That's what you want, isn't it?

Uh-huh.

You're driving to the coast? Man, if I had any less responsibility I'd go with you.

You'd be welcome.

Right now we need to pay up here and get out before Betty makes us order lunch.

With dispatch they did vacate the diner and strode the walk around to where the '42 waited. There were no spectators.

Norm rode low in his seat directing Robin to hit the open road. Ten minutes out of town he abruptly called to hold up. Robin thought he might need to relieve himself. But Norm stepped away and firmly shut the door to lean in through the open window. This is where we part, young fella.

Right here? Robin cut the engine to better hear.

Best of luck.

Do I just keep heading down this route?

As far as the pavement. This time of day and in this truck you'll not have much trouble. The constable is pretty well always east of town in the afternoons. Just before you get to Consul — that's about two hours ahead — go north on the last sideroad to the right. You'll be going up toward Cypress Hills. Take that road until you get to the park gates. You might have to cut yourself through or maybe ford a stream off the side or something. Inside there's a ranger's track going east-west. It's pretty rough but you can make it if you take it slow. In a little while you'll be on open range. Pretty wild in places. Watch out for the occasional fence. There aren't many but there are a few and they might surprise you. Find granaries and barns and outhouses to park behind. There might be a customs outpost at Govenlock. That's fifty miles west. Don't go near it if you can. Keep going along these paths until well past that until you hit a main. There'll hardly be any-body on it. Then go south to the turnoff for the States and then west again. Route Thirteen and then it turns into the Five-Oh-One, I think. Keep going as long as your fuel holds out.

Norm struck the bed tank sharp with a hard fist and lis-tened to the resonation with authority. Sounds like you got plenty so you won't have to veer south and find a gas station for a good long time. If at all.

That's how I figured it.

Smart kid. Anyway sooner or later you'll be on highways so only travel at night. Too bad you look so young. Get going at dark and quit no later than dawn every day.

I'd planned on that.

The next RCMP detachment is Foremost. That's in Alberta. Avoid the place. They got a dinky little stagnant lake close by and the mosquitos are bad even at this time of year. Keep south as much as possible. Say hello to the folks at Manyberries. Bound to be somebody there who remembers me.

Okay ...

Norm gave a cold look into the beyond and held a splayed hand toward Robin. Look at that. Steady.

It sure is.

Forty-five years old this summer. I got all my faculties about
me.

For sure. Robin pondered, not sure what to say next. So ...
I sure hope you're okay to get back to Chuck's place.

Norm's look silenced. Robin came aware that he no longer
heard the starling chitter at the roadside and there was a decided hush through the heavy-bearded flax sheaves thronging in
wind close by.

Never you mind about anybody else's troubles.

Anything you say, Norm.

The gaunt-eyed man turned and gestured north. He smiled.
Next stop Alberta.

Robin knew now to start the '42 and put it in gear. Though
he had determined not to allow sentiment at least until the
crescendo of his journey and had only known the man scarcely
a day, Norm's fading rear-view image caught at his throat.

• • •

Robin's mind cleared as he sped along the paved road. There
was much to consider. Oncoming cars were rare but they still
had to be assessed. In that region at that time of year to avoid
an overheated engine it was necessary to clear a crust of dead
and near-dead locusts from the grille every forty miles or so.
This he did a couple of times before he was back down to a
slower pace on gravel.

In time there approached a spur north that looked non-used
and by its roughness and ethereal direction slightly intimidating. Robin ignored his reluctance and pulled off and over a
short rise. The track levelled through rolling fields running to
distant high hills, glens, and straths, which he understood to be
the great land interruption of the Cyprus Hills reserve.

He reasoned that this had been his plan all along and all the subterfuge and routing he had done and had been instructed to do were in fact what he truly wanted. After a mile or so a bisection of roadway east to west allowed him to once again point toward his destination. By late afternoon he paused by a slough and found nearby a pump well with a near full priming bucket. Slaked and head-wetted with iron-cold water, Robin looked around and understood that the wheat fields would soon end. Though grain stands waved blond manes in the wind, he saw that there were fewer gopher holes. He de-kernelled a flaxen head between two hands, blew away the chaff and tossed the mess into his mouth, chewing until it was a savoury gum. For three seasons he'd observed crops' eternal green-to-gold transfiguration and proudly felt himself an element of that molecular dirt-seed-light-moisture food system.

Chew.

Swallow.

He gazed out across the wavering plains, then slid behind the wheel again.

The going over land and dust was tough with chasms and dirt pitfalls. There were diversions occasionally over raw grassland in the shadow of the ominous grey-green risings to the north that spoke of breaks and creek-cuts dangerous to his progress.

Near nightfall Robin was on the verge of finishing his transit across uncharted terrain and he ditched the '42 down into a wheat grass cut. With satisfaction he munched on the cookies he'd packed and the thermos water still drinkable and sleeping-bagged down in the truck bed.

There had been rain some days before. The air vectored with flighty spots of light in the last amber sun-glance across the meadow. He was adept at mosquito murder and handled fly transgression with humanity at first and dead dispatch later on. No-see-ums presented a particular madness that defeated even his farmhand seasoning. The zipped sleeping bag was hot but the alternative was welt bites.

After fitful semi-conscious swatting to capacity he eschewed any idea of further slumber and got going as the first orange line exhibited itself down east. The land turned shadowy red as he manoeuvred over ever more uneven ground. He stopped on a ridge to observe a lonely north-south main line. After a time one vehicle streaked along, two miles distant, so that only metal glints and a dust-tail revealed its progress.

When all was again solitary he eased the truck across the scrub and into the roadbed south to emerge from range land. The gravelled main soon led past abandoned buildings upon one of which was nailed a well-made sign:

Closed til Eternity
See Ya Then

He motored alone all the way to a right turn onto the forlorn final stretch of Saskatchewan Route Thirteen. There remained just a straight throw through cattle-dominated terrain. Such relative ease it was to drive deserted rocky highway, the blessed vibration from stones through tire rubber, up tie rods and steer column to vertebra to scapulae along metacarpal to distal phalanx and skull, a balm this truck had always given him. Ditches and sloughs either side accommodated flights of every duck and migratory bird to launch into infinite fetches up and out to oblivion aside Robin's continued westward lam.

The Envy of Every Decent Man

THE '42 RUMBLED HAPPILY ALONG THE HIGHWAY through seemingly eternal prairie sameness. The occasional opposing car was not such an alarm as Robin had feared. The anonymity of a pickup truck, no matter how vintage, on a lonely field-bound road. Hat pulled low. No hint of awareness from oncoming drivers that he might not belong just as they saw him.

No let-up of vigilance however. Barrelling into a point of lost existence in the forward vista, he saw a glint in the rearview. Something in him insisted on an interruption of the truck's comforting vibration.

He pulled over and scouted around. No presence behind. The vast beyond ahead betrayed no approaches but just as his alarm lowered there was a further rearward flit of reflection. The sharpness of it made him think of a newer non-farm vehicle, which in this region would most likely mean police.

Not far down the track was an approach off the highway over a near-buried cattle grate. He crossed the ditch and mounted the slight bank. There was a scent of manure and heat rose from the wavy stalks. Far off in another field a cattle herd reposed.

No amount of slit-eyed staring into the distance could determine for him whether or not a threat of discovery lay in the roadway five or more miles in the offing. While he deliberated, a rumbling low-bed materialized behind and dusted by, passing so fast and abrupt that Robin could not glimpse a driver. Its bed was loaded with feed. The hay harvest was happening in a rush.

All over the prairies farmers were working furiously. Robin felt this urgency and alike felt he was morally remiss in not being back there with them to swathe and combine, run dump truck aside the spewing hoppers, and transport grain to silo elevator and railcar to get food to the world.

A swig from the water can. A check of the oil. A topping of the radiator and gas tank. Then he was off to the side and away from the main across rough pasture of cow-pie and sedge, dodging the bigger clumps of buffalo grass until he found a discernible track suitably aimed. Having farmed but never ranched Robin knew only general things about cattle ranges and the roads that crisscrossed them but put his faith in the perfect direction of west-northwest that this particular trail took him.

The going was slow to the point of disappointment. Any speed achieved was interrupted by bounced impacts of head into cab roof and thighs trenching seat springs. Progressively muddy ditches presented challenges of judgment and daring. Robin surmised that the nearing hills had caught significant rainfall in the past few days and slightly feared a washout scenario or an irretrievable immersion into sucking mire from which the only escape would involve a tow vehicle.

Dusk came almost without notice. A gulp down of the left-over stuffs he'd packed and those he'd been given sufficed. He bedded semi-secreted behind a feed shed. The shed was empty so he reasoned that the area was not currently grazed.

This night the bugs were as persistent as they had been on the last but fatigue sailed him past their salvoes. He hurled into unconsciousness within an instant of closing eyelids.

He even slept past first light, rubbing crystals from his face as sunshine flowed into the truckbed.

A drink of water and check of the oil now took on utter routine. He was back in motion as daytime took full hold of the uneven green-to-grey-to-brown vista. Hours of travel revealed no changes in this landscape and neither did he see another person or even any sign aside from the occasional disused outbuilding.

Stopping for a water break in mid-afternoon he heard a yowl and then a caterwaul from somewhere off the trail and strode a hundred yards toward a discernible wrinkle in the ground. Sure enough, a calf was stuck in a cleave of hard dirt cut from a washout route and greased with loose enough mud so as to make the creature's efforts at freedom a flailing, messily futile affair.

Robin deduced that though the animal had clearly strayed from wherever its herd might be, ranchers would doubtless be somewhere approaching. He turned and strode back toward the '42.

Bawl.

He kept walking.

Bawl.

At the cab he whipped back the seat and gripped the coil of tow rope.

The biggest livestock entity he'd ever wrangled was a froward rooster who'd been brutalized for some reason to the point where the male presence of any species impelled it to attack with all its beak and claw. Robin bore the forearm and shin scars to prove he'd tried the bird's territorial dominance. For this mission he had in mind a particular strategy to loosen the animal without coming in range of any kind of injury. He also worked over mentally just how he might manage not to become mud-caked head to foot as was the creature presently.

He tried what had formed in his mind while fetching the rope. Then a combination of that idea and forceful physicality involving attempts to grasp the barely emerged prickets on the wrenching head. Ultimately it was a general grapple of boy-on-struggling-junior-bovine in a mud-wrestle spectacle that he was only slightly less glad no one witnessed than he was disappointed that his clothes and body would require such great amounts of washing.

It was nonetheless the sought-for outcome when the animal jerked free and galloped up and out of the trench with accompanied mud jets. The splattering messed his hair but he took philosophical pride at having relieved the suffering of at least one fellow creature of the world. Striding back to the truck and lurching he knew the effort had sapped him and he was utterly filthy. Before sliding behind the wheel he threw a tarp over the upholstery and wiped hands on his soiled denim.

Despite the dirt, the episode took him out of himself sufficiently to forget who he was and what he was doing. For a few miles he was oblivious. After he'd found washwater at the bottom of a deep cut and stripped off to get the dirt from his clothes and out of his hair he realized a tinglesome exhilaration. It was an odd feeling. He felt unworthy of the reward. He wandered for a time among the low scrub aside the trickling creek.

After a dip in the deeper part of the stream he felt a peculiar presence on a section of thigh covered by his sodden underwear. Pulling it away he discovered as black a leech attached there as he had imagined in any childhood horror. He had heard of this kind of thing but never experienced it and only passingly understood a proper removal procedure. Direct extraction by way of fretful yanking was out, as he recalled someone saying. Rummaging in the tool box for what he hoped was a near forgotten plastic lighter he tried not to acknowledge the disgusting sensation of a gelatinous parasite sucking so close to his crotch. At last he found the lighter and with still-wet fingers flicked it several times to get a flame. The smell of burning organism and the sting of rising heat on his skin did not deter him. The icky creature curled and let go.

Careful not to get close to underbrush or water weed he returned to the stream to scrub himself twice-over with a fragment of soap, then rinsed off and towelled and broke out clean clothes from the kit bag.

Back behind the wheel the sun was low.

The approach of several low structures in the forward gloom was welcome, particularly because of the character of cloud cover in the upwind distance. Ninety-nine percent chance of rain was his judgment. Robin pulled into a levelled area with tool shed and sty still standing and a barn with a partially collapsed roof, its wide door swung open and various outbuildings near falling to the ground. Rock-and-mortar foundational remnants of a ranch house were detectable amid the general decay. Without pause he edged the pickup to the wavering door and nudged a fender to open it farther. The vehicle fit neatly into the part of the barn floor clear enough to drive upon but covered still by the best part of the remaining roof.

He switched off in time to hear the first notes of thunder, the day being still light enough for him not to have noticed the lightning. By the time he'd munched through the last of the food — a near-bad roast beef sandwich with too little mustard followed by one of the two oatmeal cookies left — the atmosphere had turned sombre and frequent fork flashes shock-veined the sky.

For a time he sat in semi-dark and tried to detect any redolent spirit the wood and rust and forgotten shreds might hold. Though there was little if any pong of animal agriculture he did develop an odd scalp tightening and unexplained inner awe looking across the yard through glassless windows toward where the house once stood. Someone had turned this land long ago and marshalled the necessary beasts to create a living. Being of the practical land himself and thus resistant to metaphysical sentiment he did not ponder hard. He could not, however, resist a slight shudder.

After an initial torrent the rain settled to a steady thrum. He knew it would be a damp night regardless of such good fortune finding shelter. A rearrangement of available detritus — a couple of broken sawhorses, rusty metal chair, shattered wooden packing crate — allowed him to stretch on the truck seat with his feet out the driver's door resting on an improvised construction. Due to his now nightly bone fatigue Robin's sleep progressed peacefully despite rumbled intrusion and dripping columns with frequent stark bolt flickers of nature's light switch.

With dawn there was quiet. Sun shafts pierced the cracked roof from a clear sky. Later in the morning a motor sound woke him. Tensed and ready, he raised an eye above the dash to peer through the slits in the walls enough to see a truck wobble through the yard. Hidden as he was there was no indication by tone of engine or direction of steer that his presence had been detected. Nor by the slant light and rain-washed surface would the driver likely see the fresher ruts his tires had made in barnyard dirt.

The low-bed rig receded into the eastward prairie. He found his hands trembling and his breath short. This was private land after all. He held no firm understanding as to the seriousness of trespass.

The last oatmeal cookie comprised breakfast and he was glad to find the ancient outhouse operational as last night's sandwich acted up boisterous in his guts. Once free of this minor distress he continued with the morning vehicular ablutions: oil check and top-up; fuel; radiator check; coolant levels. On this morning Robin took a long moment to consider the tires. One of them — rear passenger side — was visibly down. He checked the spare to see if there was as much pressure as when he'd brought everything up to travel standard back in the Scott machine shop. There was. Nevertheless … besides the loneliness he was beginning to feel out here in the forgotten nothingness of ruins and abandoned lives, he would be needing service station facilities sometime soon to make sure everything kept running. Not to mention the terrible fact that he was out of food.

He was encouraged to find that after leaving the forlorn ranch the road improved. That day he drove with increased determination to see civilization at least before daylight faded. Before noon he reached a junction. The gravel main ran perpendicular to the direction he had been travelling and a continuation of his chosen lane meant crossing the right of way by means of a couple of crude culverts. He debated. Right or left meant happening onto people sooner than later. This had become a big draw in his mental auditorium. A great speech was made in his mind about the joys of being part of humanity again. Still. These directions were not west — an opposing voice insisted — and as such were counterproductive. Waste of gasoline and time. Perhaps even a path to failure.

Robin tested the water jug in the cab. One quarter left. He had another full one in the back sitting among the three empties he'd drained over the trek so far. He pulled the growling truck off the plain and onto the wide dusty road and paused. Heat from the gravel bed instantly rose and got him sweaty. A calculation of how much water he would need for two more days' travel took a few minutes and at the end he'd forgotten how he deduced if he even knew that two days would be enough to arrive somewhere he could eat food and get air in his tires and perchance get clean. Even sleep in a bed perhaps.

Amid this pondering a grit-spewing semi-trailer rig crested from the south and closed with speed enough to force a reactive decision. Robin revved the engine, popped the clutch, and jolted across the road to land back onto the faint but passable track he'd been on for what felt like most of his life.

An hour of determined teamstering over reasonable but rising topography had him pause at a high ridge and locate in the hazed lower distance the grid-image of a settlement dead ahead. An instant lightening of his heart radiated to his throat and down his arms and wrists. A continued push all day toward this unknown but so welcome sight of a town would have him before nightfall at least getting a cup of coffee in a diner. Hamburger. Fries and a piece of pie. He forced himself to step out to stand and stretch. Urinate. Drink a sparing single gulp of water and flex his hands before jumping back in the cab and lurching the '42 downward toward this welcome burg.

In a short life on the prairie he'd experienced the optical illusion of time and distance being fluid quantities, but comprehension of just how far this destination was near beggared Robin's patience. Hard driving all the rest of the day got him nearer but nowhere close to there. The light failed and the track, though improving, seemed to go on without end. Even when he began to pass occupied farms along the way it seemed he would never actually arrive.

Distracted by hunger and expectation, he did not notice, even as he flicked the truck lights on, that he was travelling on a well-used roadway with traffic both oncoming and rearward.

Finally it was in a near swoon that he pulled up on a wide-buildinged thoroughfare and his headlights told of an avenue named Raspberry. After a left on Bullberry he hit Cactus Berry, followed by Saskatoon Street. Down one way he saw a couple of vehicles parked in front of a hotel-like structure with one lighted window in front. A restaurant sign said "Ranchmen's Inn." As he pulled over and braked Robin realized he was barely awake and only hunger was poking him conscious enough to navigate. He had presence of mind enough to park acceptably then switch off and kill the lights. Then he was unconscious.

• • •

Tap tap tap. You awake? Tap tap tap. Why you sleeping?

Robin drifted through a nebula, striding foamy surf and windblown seaside. The dreamed sun on his forehead smarted. He jerked awake to unstick his face from the steering wheel. A man's knuckles on the '42's door frame in the dark were rousing him.

Hey. You're not Orville.

Uh ...

I thought you were Orville.

No. I'm not Orville.

Whattya doing in Orville's truck then? The man stood back, his head swivelling to and fro at the properties of the pickup. Well. Actually. Maybe not.

This is my truck. Robin gestured toward the Ranchmen's Inn sign. Can I get some food here?

It's like Orville's but not. His is a thirty-nine Ford.

· This is a forty-two Chev. Is this place open?

Oh here? Yeah you can get food. Heh heh. Tomorrow morning.

Robin noticed that the sign and window had gone dark and wondered fatally how long he'd been unconscious.

The man standing aside wavered and stifled a laugh. You know what time it is?

No.

A look at a watch. One a.m.

Whoa.

You're not gonna get anythin' to eat 'til mornin'. This place opens up at six.

Oh.

Hey fella … The man leaned in and Robin near gagged at a wafting toxic halitosis. You got a drink on ya?

A drink? I got water.

That's not what I'm looking for …

I haven't got much.

Well heck …

The man lurched off into the darkness. Robin slumped down, folded as fetal as he could on the upholstery, then bolted awake at sharp sunbeams coming low through a gap in the storefronts. A mufflerless one-ton was parking beside him. He could hardly remember where he was. All he knew was that he needed food.

Midway through bacon and eggs he drew a chuckle from the aproned matron by ordering a long stack of pancakes. Once most of the way through those her expression was mild alarm when he demanded the steak-and-eggs special. After that he drew laughter from the farmer assemblage now lining the walls of the place when he asked for another side of toast with jam and took a fifth or sixth coffee refill, chomping and gulping away in such fashion as not to allow conversation or even the basic greet niceties of standard prairie-town diner etiquette.

Hellfire, boy. Did you try the Spanish omelette?

Too foreign for him, Bill. Likes the local fare.

How was that steak, young fella?

Just fine, thanks. Robin knew to look up and smile wide. What else is good around here?

Waffles with fruit and whipped cream. My wife only lets me have it on special occasions. But you're a starving young growing boy so have at 'er, son.

I just might. Can you tell me … what's a bullberry?

Laughter all around.

You mean buffalo berry.

What's a buffalo berry?

Oh just another kind of prairie bush that gives back if you think to go out and see when the fruit develops on 'em. Mostly just a notable feature of this town where we got a street named after it.

I know. I saw.

Not from around here, huh?

Nope.

Heading somewheres?

West. Got dropped off last night. Hoping to get a bus. Is there any?

Not 'til you get to Foremost. 'Bout an hour up the road.

Oh.

Hitchin'?

Yeah.

Well. Not much traffic along this way. Might be somebody headin' out there sometime today. Want me to find out for ya?

Uh that's okay. I got a friend to call. Coming up this way from down south. Either way.

Heads swivelled as the diner door opened to let a burly man through. Whooee. That's sure a sweet-looking old-time pickup out there. Did you finally get that thirty-nine of yours fixed up, Orville?

Nope. That's not mine. Got Saskatchewan plates. It's a Chev. Must be someone visiting.

Huh.

Yeah I saw it too. Never seen that particular one around here before.

Robin took a long pull of coffee as a casual way to cover his face with something.

Must be some fella up the street doing some business or other. But ...

The three farmers got up and left.

Orville and his breakfast mate followed. Take it easy, young friend. Hope you get a ride.

Appreciate it.

Take care.

Luck.

Thanks.

Robin stretched the last inch of coffee so that all the men who'd spoken with him were gone and out of sight by the time he drank it. He rose, fishing bills out of his pocket and faced the matron.

No need, hon. Those guys got it for you.

Huh?

You impressed them with your eating abilities. Not much happens around here. They got a kick out of your killing off most of the breakfast menu.

Well. Gee.

Ha ha. You put on a good show. That's your reward.

Sure is nice of them.

He lingered at the door to just get a scan of the street but not so long that the nice lady might think he desired further conversation. Outside he swung away from where the '42 was parked. A stroll along the crumbled sidewalk and down to the dusty roadway and back up a wooden walk that connected to still more wizened concrete. None of the diner men were in evidence from what the corners of his eyes could collect. He crossed the street, pulling his hat down a little lower to shade the still-low sun. A tractor prattled near, going slow, and a hay truck pulled around a corner to head opposite. He stepped back along the shaded side and saw how escape would best be done. At the block end he recrossed and went down the only other street to a gap where a supposed alleyway existed but was simply the empty backyard of a semi-active business. A leap over two low fences and then the gap toward the street took him to where the nose of the '42 poked near.

For good measure he crouch-walked low to slide into the passenger side. Without closing the door he peered through the side and rear windows to be satisfied there were no people so close by that they might notice the start-up. He assumed the arm-out farmhand driver's posture position and hit the starter. Backing out he was careful not to let the passenger door swing too violent and shut it perfect with forward movement. He took a short ride down the street and a hard right.

The street almost instantly led onto open highway. Robin dusted fast due west on what he knew was a road so good he would not be able to enjoy it for more than a mile or two. Ahead he spied indeterminate vehicle clouds that no doubt contained earnest workers who ninety-nine percent of the time would mind their own business. He pondered each potential turnoff and possible dodge.

Amidst these deliberations a ruffling vibration issued from behind and the wheel in his hands wrenched and yawed unnaturally. Though travelling at speed he managed to coax the fishtailing '42 down from its forty-five mile per hour headlong to a manageable drift to the side and a skidding halt just off the right of way but not quite into the wide ditch. So occupied with piloting the descent he forgot to take it out of gear and when backing off the clutch lurched the truck into a stall. He sat and breathed deep.

By the time another vehicle had rumbled up he was out of the cab and undoing lug nuts holding the spare. One look at the shredded rear tire remonstrated with him the folly of forgotten deflation. He understood that he'd been foolish to depend on such long-used rubber for such an arduous trip. On that score it occurred to him as he assembled the jack that in fact this beautiful truck he loved so much had not likely travelled farther away from Jimmy Scott's farm than it was right now and more likely never nearly as far. He undertook the careful repair process with this tender fact in mind.

The third vehicle to appear rolled to a gentle stop behind and as Robin began the up and down handle-pump raising of the body away from the gravel he heard its door swing open and the crunch of boot on gravel.

So it is your honey after all!

Robin was too tense to recognize the voice but saw immediately upon looking that Orville from the diner had stopped to look in on him.

Howdy.

Got some trouble?

Not really. Just a flat.

Pretty badly cut up there. The big man crouched smiling and ran a hand along the deflated tire. Not gonna salvage this one.

Wasn't much to begin with.

Naw I can see that. Not like the rest of 'er. You restore it?

I took care of it. It was kind of in original condition. Man that owned it babied it along for pretty well its whole life.

Huh. Orville peered at Robin's work. I can see you don't need mechanical help.

Nope.

But you need something … The pause in Orville's sentence was taken up by the conscious widening of his smile … Dontcha?

Not sure what you mean, sir.

Name's Orville Joyce, son. What's yours?

Robin Wallenco.

Well Robin, my boy, do you mind if I ask why a youngster like you … fourteen or fifteen —

Almost sixteen.

— is doing driving a vintage pickup across countryside where he doesn't farm local and is known in the town by absolutely nobody?

Well I … Robin continued with the repair. I come from just north of Kincaid.

Uh-huh. I know the area.

And I'm heading west.

I can see that. How far?

Well. BC if I can.

How far in BC?

The coast.

You got a fair ways to go. You come a fair ways too, considering the kind of roads you must have travelled. I assume you're mostly driving rangeland ruts. Likely nobody would bother you on those.

That's right.

What are you doing for food and water?

I ran out of grub a couple of days ago.

I saw you reload.

Huh … yeah. Thanks for paying for breakfast.

Don't mention it.

The repair was well along even though Robin had had to practically stand on the lug wrench with two of the pneumatic-tightened bolts. As the last one cracked its way loose both became aware of a car having come up the road eastward and making a large U-turn to swing in in front. As the dust blew off, Robin tensed at seeing that it was a blinking police cruiser. Orville stood and regarded the officer's slow stride to the cowling of the '42.

Constable.

Hello there. Orville, is it?

That's right.

And whose fine wreck is this?

Robin was ready with an answer but Orville spoke first: I finally fixed that old relic my dad left me and now it's sprung a blowout. Wouldn't ya know it?

Huh.

Good thing my man here was following along. Had the tools ready and everything.

Robin kept his head down and hat low and worked intently as a hired hand would. He made a show of lifting the spare onto the wheel and spinning it for effect.

The constable sidled behind and peered at the licence plate. I appreciate you making sure it was registered and all.

Wouldn't think of driving it illegal.

But you're not supposed to register an Alberta vehicle in Saskatchewan you know.

Oh it's kind of a nostalgia thing. It's where it was from in the first place. Anyways we're kind of on the border here any-way you know. My dad never did register it any other place.

Well … Don't do it again, okay? It's technically illegal although I know half this town does it all the time. That doesn't make it any more right.

Understood.

I'm afraid you better. Next time I'm gonna have to write you up on it.

You won't have to. This baby's mostly for show anyway. It'll stay on the farm.

Good.

Both stood back to observe Robin as he tightened the spare evenly with half-turn gradations on opposite bolts as he'd been taught. The constable looked up the road and then down. You okay here?

My man is on the job right now as you can see. He's a good kid with a wrench.

Yeah well … Get it done fast as you can. You're nearly in the way.

We'll be gone momentary.

Robin only regained full breathing as the cruiser blinked off its cherry-top and moved away. He lowered the jack to get the tire on the ground for the final turns of the lugs.

Whew. Orville leaned against the back fender. That was a lot of explaining.

I sure appreciate it. Robin force-tightened the last bolt and reattached the hubcap with several palm-force blows. I hope he believed it.

Hardly matters after we get you and your rig off the main road. If you care to you can follow me. I got some parts at my place might help you out. Tires too.

Um …

You'll need a re-up of water soon, eh. And oil. Have you got oil?

Some.

Can't carry too much with these old geezers.

She's been using a bit but not a lot.

Wait'll you get on those long climbs up the Rockies.

Yeah. I guess.

Lookit, just slip in behind me. It's five miles northwest. Not too much off your route.

Okay.

All right.

Robin packed his tools.

Orville's spread was the first grain outfit Robin had seen since leaving his transit across the open-graze lands. He followed across an extensive yard with numerous machines and into a Quonset hangar of such immensity he was not sure he'd ever seen the like. He parked beside a combine. He looked around at the various grinders and lathes and tool arrays with compressor welder lift and every other mechanical-working device imaginable. Orville strode to a washstand to run water and returned with a glass each.

They sat on the running board of the '42 and drank.

By the way. What were you gonna tell him?

Huh?

The cop. I could see you were getting set to start babbling.

Robin considered for a moment and decided to let all go. I was gonna ... I was gonna say I was sent for a combine part you could only get at Foremost. I heard they got big dealerships there. And something like my dad was broke and didn't have any other vehicle and couldn't afford to leave the farm because my mom was sick.

And how much of that might be at least a bit true?

None.

None? You got a dad, don'tcha?

Yeah. But not here.

And a mom?

Yes but not here either.

I'm guessing then that that there's why you have to get to BC.

Yup.

All the way to the coast you say?

All the way to Vancouver Island then maybe across as far as I can go.

Ha! No lack of ambition.

I just have to get out there.

Well you might go far … making stuff up like you do. Heh. That was some fine invention there by the way, kid. I just hope you don't end up in a jail somewhere if somebody checks out your spiel.

I guess.

They drank in a silence broken only by the contraction ticks of their respective trucks' cooling engines.

Orville knocked knuckles against the fender. You know how rare this vehicle is?

Yes.

Know the history?

They stopped building trucks for civilians a few months after the States got into the war.

Right you are. Right after Pearl Harbor. They might not have made more than a few hundred before they switched to military motors to fight the Japs and Jerrys.

My friend told me all that stuff.

Is it a January or a February?

February.

You know for sure?

The VIN number is pretty near to the end of the series. Jimmy looked it up. He thought it was one of the last off the line.

And it's not a half-ton, is it?

Not exactly sure.

Might be a three quarter. Some of them were. And it's a long box. Good for sleeping. Does it have six-bolt wheels?

Yeah.

Might be a heavy duty version. You'd have to look up the model numbers and all that. Doesn't make much difference though.

Not to me.

Atta boy. Does the speedometer work?

Yup.

How fast you had it up to?

Fast as I've got it going on blacktop was near fifty. Not sure it can do any better.

With those beat-up bias plies you got on 'er I wouldn't recommend it.

I've been taking it easy.

Good idea. But I might have something for you.

Orville rose, laid his empty glass on the hood of his pickup, and stepped toward a canvas silhouette near the back of the hangar. A considerable puff of dust accompanied the jerked removal of the tarp and as Robin expected, an old pickup reposed there.

This here's what they were talking about back at the café. My dad's thirty-nine Ford.

She's pretty.

Not as nice as yours. But I been hoping to get 'er back to cherry condition some time or other.

Well. Looks like you have the stuff you need to do it. Is this all for your farm?

Oh yeah. But I take other work too. Welding and repairs mostly. That's why I think I can help you out. Orville gripped a pair of tires leaning against the truck body. These might be too big a profile …

Maybe not. I modified the wheel-wells some.

Well, let's try 'em.

In the course of a heavily industrial half-day man and boy transposed all tires on the '42 from the used products Robin had started out with to the near-new copies Orville had intended for the restoration of his own. Later they replaced oil and filters, gas cap, windshield wiper blade, and headlight bulbs. Orville topped up the truck and the bed transfer tank with farm gas and loaded two-gallon cans of motor oil under the seat. Leaving Robin to work on a full cleaning of the bed and interior Orville left the hangar to return with a plate of sandwiches and a battered Styrofoam cooler to keep them in. He and Robin ate as afternoon heat rose outside and wafted into the work space on a lazy breeze.

I sure can't pay you for all this just now.

You don't have to anytime.

I will but I just don't know when.

Suit yourself.

I sure am lucky running into you, Orville.

Think nothing of it, son. Someday you'll come across somebody who needs something.

I guess that's how it works.

In a perfect world. Orville paused, chewing, and stood up. I'd invite you to stay awhile if you're tired but I'm kind of keeping you a secret.

Yes, sir.

My wife doesn't need anything more on her mind and the kids are bound to blab enough to get word around to that constable we conned this morning and there'd be hell to pay.

I see it.

So I'm recommending you get going while there's still good hours of light left. You could hustle out over a track across my land and then through neighbour Phil's place. Orville stepped to the entrance and pointed off to the northwest. There. I'll show you on a map. He found a folded map on the workbench and spread it across the cowling of the '42. We're right here. He pointed with an edge of his sandwich. You can make it to there by nightfall without travelling any roads anybody will care about.

Uh-huh.

There's an auto court just past this big lake that lets people park their trailers and vans. You can probably slip in near dark, get some sleep, and use their facilities in the morning. Continue along on this here line for a good part of the way clear across. You'll come out to a main route north of Milk River and then you can keep going across here to near Cardston. This way you more or less bypass any place that has police. That's important.

Sure is.

You're gonna be crossing more open range. Not too many people around. Are you ready for that?

Uh-huh.

You got enough fuel between your tank and all that forty gallons you got in the reserve. But after Cardston I don't know what you're going to do. It's all blacktop highway up the foothills and into the Rockies.

I'll figure something.

You'll have to. Be a shame to come all that way and have the Mounties take it away from you.

I can't thank you enough.

Kid. Orville stood back and shook his head smiling. You're the envy of every decent man. The thought of just picking up and driving out in your personal vehicle for parts little known.

No particular schedule. Fate dictating every single day. Even for a little while it would suit one man or another at some part of his life.

Well. I wish it was fun as you make it out.

Ha. Just remember stuff, kid. Hang on to the things you see and the people you meet and the times you have. There'll be dark days but there's always gonna be light too. By the looks of what you've done so far you might always have an interesting life.

It was on this note or something similar that Robin started up and backed the '42 slowly out of the hangar. He slid it into forward gear and waved goodbye. The afternoon had turned hot and more humid than he'd been used to on the flatter prairie. He surmised that this might have been due to the preponderance of lakes now decorating the landscape.

He made the overnight auto camp stop Orville had outlined just as dusk turned to complete dark and spent the night in the truck bed snug in his sleeping bag surprisingly free of mosquito interference. In the morning a ten-year-old girl — he deduced she was a child of the resort — asked him for a one dollar fee. Knowing such a youngster would not likely suspect his relative youth enough to raise undue attention he gladly paid extra to launder his clothes in the washroom and take a joyous long shower.

Progress from here proved better than over the less tamed Cyprus lands. The track was more distinct. There were even serviceable if precarious woodbridge crossings between occasional grain stands and over the considerable water courses now in plenitude across the countryside. He stopped for meals and refuelling on the two occasions where fences presented an unavoidable delay.

It was his policy to try to find gaps either intended or accidental but on this route he found the barriers both stoutly

installed and all-encompassing. He surmised that the ranchers
knew the access and egress of each respective range and kept
this information to themselves. Accordingly he congratulated
himself on having brought along the proper equipment to both
disassemble the wires to allow passage and the pliers and extra
barb stock to correct the condition.

A full day's travel wherein he began to catch himself forgetting what he had been before and any kind of life that preceded
this headlong transit overland saw him approach a paved north–
south artery and evidence of a city distant to the left. As he came
to the thoroughfare from high ground an odd compendium of
vehicles and individuals became visible in a crook in the road
where there was what looked to him an impromptu campsite.

He forded a shallow creek, then followed a scant foot trail.
Then the foot trail petered out and he found he was instantly
amidst the assembly. It appeared to be a near-carnival atmosphere. He was seized by an urge to stop and idle.

What commandeered Robin's attention mostly were the
girls in flowing dresses moving about barefoot, their smiles a
surprise gift. The men took little notice, busy as they were sitting around campfires and hauling wood and water. Not a few
strummed guitars and pounded drums. He circuited the camp
slowly and saw that the nearby highway was populated by similar revellers with signs out advertising to prospective hitchhike
rides where they would wish to go.

Seeing finally that an opportunity was at hand to secrete
himself and the '42 for the night and enjoy human company too
he slid the truck between a beflowered Cadillac and a squiggly-
painted Volkswagen van. As the engine's rumble subsided he
received the tuneful orientation of the place. He stepped out
stretching and leaned against the grille to observe the passersby
who by turn duly surveyed him.

Cool ride, man.

Sweet. Farm contemporary, dude. Smart.

Welcome, feed-and-seed boy.

Headin' out to Californey there, Tom Joad?

Long way from Oklahoma, huh.

Hey it's John Steinbeck, the early years!

Far out, man.

Goin' to a car show?

Too much.

Hey where'd you find Grampa's truck?

Robin chuckled at it all and as it kept coming understood that though a figure of soft ridicule he was likely as safe from detection or interference in this slant community as he needed to be. As darkness came he relaxed at how perfectly the '42 nestled among the other rolling stock and by association with the gaudily decorated heaps attracted little relative notice.

He took food from the cooler and sidled toward one of the fires. Here again he was gratified to find that no particular note was taken of him and the conversation and general music was shared with a liberating sense of non-propriety. He sat and smiled at everyone.

Hey, is that a ham sandwich? The cotton-clad girl aside him leaned close and peered at his supper.

Yup.

I'm reeeeeeally hungry.

Well have some. He tore the bread in two and handed off the half.

Wow cool. She jawed into the sandwich with shark-like voracity. They're cooking up lentils over by the van but I can't wait.

Well. You're welcome.

My name's Aldis.

Robin.

Cool name.

So's yours.

Yum. Good sanny. Did you make it?

Nope. A farmer … or his wife more likely. Gave me a whole bunch. And a cooler with an ice pack to go with it.

Just gave it to you?

That's right.

Maybe the world is changing after all.

Huh?

Give what you can. A man with holes in his T-shirt spoke as he handed out paper plates with what looked to Robin to be bean stew on them. Take what you need. It's the vibe we're trying to spread inside this capitalist planetary prison, man.

Whoa …

Whoa is right. Want some lentil?

Uh sure.

The mass tasted of an odd spice Robin suspected he'd either never had or perhaps had had only once and not enough to know what it was.

How's the curry? Did I get it right?

Fine.

Not too bland?

Kinda hot.

Perfect.

Aldis finished her half-sandwich and took a bite of lentils. It's great, Percival.

Thanks, kiddo. Where's your cousin?

Oh Karen? I don't know. Said she was going to try to score some dope or something.

Okay you guys do what you want but you just got here. You should know. The cops come through like about noon every day.

Oh?

So make sure you don't have anything on you.

Okay.

So far we've been pretty lucky. But if anybody gets busted they'll roust the rest of us for sure.

Okay.

So who's the new guy?

His name's Robin. Like the bird. Aldis spoke with a rapture that surprised Robin. He's captain of that beautiful old pickup truck.

Oh. Hey cool, man. Where you from?

Well right now I'm from south Saskatchewan.

Where you headed?

Vancouver Island.

Whoa. West. That's cool.

You heading north?

For now. Far away from south as possible, anyway.

Aldis threw an arm around Robin and nudged her nose close to his cheek. Isn't he cute?

Kinda young for you, Aldis. A woman had appeared on the edge of the firelight. Unless he's going to give us a ride.

Are you going to give us a ride, Robin?

He shifted so as to disengage enough for comfort but not so much as to give what he feared would be taken as rejection. I don't know. Where're you going?

Aldis laid her head on his shoulder.

The woman strode to a seat beside her. Montreal.

Oh. Well. I guess you didn't hear. I'm going west.

No I didn't hear. I was too busy getting these. She opened a hand to reveal three homemade cigarettes.

Percival leaned acutely in the firelight to see what was contained in her curled hand. Yay, Karen. Nice going. Let's get lit up, people, shall we?

A murmur of approval circuited the firelight and after Karen pocketed one of the joints the remainders were lit up and distributed in each direction. When the proffered smoking roll arrived at Robin he demurred. No thanks.

That's cool. Not into it?

I don't even smoke real cigarettes.

They're way more harmful for you.

Well. Whatever.

Karen drew on the smoke she held and expelled its exhaust slowly into the atmosphere above the firelight. What are you into, truckboy?

Into? I don't know. Driving, I guess.

Driving. Like polluting the atmosphere?

I don't drive unless I have to.

Have to. Why do you have to? Why does anybody have to?

Well it's kind of the way the world works. Isn't it? Right now anyway.

Right now.

He's got a point, man. Change has to be fundamental.

Whatever that means. But let the boy tell. Why do you drive?

I'm heading out to see my dad.

Where's your dad?

I don't exactly know. I'm hoping my mom does.

Oho. Family drama. Does your daddy love you?

The taunting tenor of Karen's interrogative gave Robin cause to shift feet and stare into the crackly fire without words.

Have no illusions, kid. Percival finished a long expel of marijuana smoke and shook his head. Your papa doesn't like you. Nobody's does. They see the hair. Hear the music. They think we're all some kind of deviant to be stamped out. That's why I'm not going to 'Nam. My dad's a vet. From D-Day on he walked from France all the way to Berlin. Saw lots of guys die.

To him that's the way of the world. War. Everybody should do it, he thinks. And the generals in Saigon. They're all from World War Two. Think a hundred guys a day is okay for casualties. They're killing dozens a minute over there because they don't understand jungle or French-Asian food. No idea how sacred a village water buffalo is. They don't understand nationalist guerrillas who dig tunnels and swear to die repelling the invader, whoever they are. They think burger and fries is a good meal. Bowl of rice is crap. They don't know how long this could last. It's already longer than they fought in Europe and no end in sight. They want their own offspring to suffer and the wildest of us to die. Think we deserve it. Hope it cleanses the generation somehow. Breaks us. Gets the ya-yas out.

Though taken aback by the grave tone the talk had taken, Robin was glad for a conversational change. Did you get drafted?

Not yet but it was coming. I'll tell you one thing. Me and Beckie. We ain't never going back. We packed up the van. Drove up to the border. Answered all their questions. They can wage war all they want to wage wherever and for whatever they want to wage it. We ain't never going back … Day I crossed that Canada line was the best day of my life. Soon as I get a part for that VW there we're getting farther and farther away too.

You need a part?

Master cylinder is gone on the thing. No brakes. Had to nurse it into here on the handbrake and damn near crashed as it was.

When will it come?

Supposed to be tomorrow if the guy in Milk River is to be believed. I don't think he likes me too much. But I paid cash to have it put on a bus over from Lethbridge.

You got tools?

Some.

Well if it gets in tomorrow early enough maybe I can give you a hand.

That'd be great.

I'm thankful for the stew.

Oh hey. More where that came from if you're still hungry.

No thanks. But there's always breakfast.

Ha ha …

You guys are such bullshitters. Karen's ire seemed undiminished by the substance she'd been smoking. Everybody's running from something. You're fleeing the war which makes you at least slightly smart. You're trying to find your dad? Come on. What are you running from, kid?

Well. I wrecked my friend's rod weeder.

What, pray tell, is a rod weeder?

It's an attachment you drag behind a big tractor. A bunch of thick arms push down this one-inch thick steel rod under the soil about four inches and it pulls out all the weeds.

Oh. Sounds destructive. How'd you wreck it more?

Well I didn't actually wreck it. I weeded a whole field for a whole day with about two feet of the rod missing off one end. The darn field has a green stripe of weeds up and down it now.

Though mentally Robin struggled to edit the explanation down to essentials, before he could finish there were titters and giggles.

Whoa … are the cops ever after you!

What a desperado!

Watch out! Serial farmer on the loose …

Jimmy didn't want me to do it over.

Who's Jimmy?

The guy whose farm I was working on. The guy who took me in a few years ago and treated me great.

Aldis shifted and took his hand. Jimmy sounds like a cool guy.

Something in the wilding direction of the night's talk let Robin consider going on past all prudence. That was the night we had to take him to the clinic for the last time.

Oh. Was he sick?

Cancer. He only lived another two weeks.

Oooh … downer.

You must be so bummed.

Heavy, man.

How do we know all this is true? How do we know this kid isn't making it all up to send us on some kind of sympathy trip?

Jeez, Karen. What's up your butt?

Robin stood. Think I'm going to get bedded down. He sighted Percival in the firelight. What time do you think that part will come in?

I'm hitching a ride down there first thing. Want to get going as early as possible, man.

Okay.

By the way. Don't know if it means anything to you. As I was saying to these two earlier … the cops do a regular patrol through here. The last couple of days it's been pretty near noon. So if you'd rather not have 'em see you …

Thanks for letting me know.

As he walked from the fireside into the dark a comfort enfolded Robin in a way unfamiliar. He knew he would have to think on his experiences here as everywhere and come to some settlement about what they meant and what he might take from them. Something about the tenor of the night and the mood of the people set him to a reflective undertaking he had never contemplated.

At the truck he eyed the starry sky for any sign of disturbance and judging it unlikely to rain pulled his bedroll from the cab and made ready to lay out in the box. A quick urination down the shrubs at the side of the draw. He brushed his teeth and spat water into darkness near the same place. Stepping back to the truck he could enjoy the low singing and guitar caresses from the campfires but felt good to be about to sleep. Behind him a step became audible in the crunchy gravel.

Hey, kid.

Yes.

Sorry I was such a bag.

By the dimness he could discern Karen as a jet silhouette against the flicker illumination of the flames and the brilliance of the night's distinct stars.

Oh that's okay.

I brought you a bottle of pop. It's my last one. She proffered a bottle he could only just see by reflections.

That's okay. I'm going to sleep now.

You sure? Here. I'll leave it for you. She stepped to the '42 and placed it on the running board.

Thanks.

It's my peace gesture. She held up two splayed fingers. Peace, man.

Peace.

It doesn't count if you don't accept my peace offering.

Oh?

No.

Well. He stepped to the bottle and held it. Thanks.

It's Orange Crush. Do you like Orange Crush?

I'm more of a root beer man myself.

Ha ha. You're funny. It's my last one.

Maybe I'll drink it for breakfast. Just brushed my teeth.

Huh. Okay.

Well. Good night.

Are you going to sleep in that thing?

Yes.

Under the stars?

Yup.

Well. Have a good time.

I'll try.

She receded so slowly to darkness he wondered if she would actually go. The strangeness of the encounter was not especially disquieting to him now that he had spent several hours in this odd camp. There was a peculiar sense of pride at interacting and being apparently accepted by such a disparate collection of road people. He stood the pop bottle on the floor of the cab and shut the door on it, then swung up into the truck bed. Shucking his shirt and jeans to roll into a pillow he cocooned inside the bedroll with a greater relief than he'd anticipated. He left the bag unzipped and open so as to easily expose a leg to the cooling night air. The faint voice and music wafting from the fireside soothed more than kept him awake and no more than one minute passed before he was drifting. If ten more seconds had gone by he would have been fully non-conscious when a warm body pressed itself into him under his crowding covers.

Uh ...

Hello, sweetie.

His alarm was attenuated by recognition of Aldis's voice. Uh ...

Did I wake you? I'm glad if I did.

He struggled to answer but found his intellectual capacity cancelled entirely by the sensual wonders of such closeness with a body he now understood was unclothed. Sensations overcame thought and the notion of speaking was so far from his ability now that he almost chuckled aloud even as her hand guided his to her most fantasied spots.

He was in confoundment at how there seemed utterly no necessity for words amid the arousal. Alternately resisting inside a moral rampart, vainly trying to at least slow the progression of the event, he also marvelled by touch at her perfect living sculpture.

The art of her.

An appreciation for so much more of the world blossomed in his consciousness. Amid the sensuous overload Robin could at least understand that this stunning time was a particular gift.

Then amid the celebration of visceral wondrousness he was startled to receive a fierce firing of affection for Aldis, who was now manoeuvring herself beneath him on the thrown-open sleeping bag. Their general heatforce ambushed him entirely and engulfed so completely with affection he nearly shed a unexpected tear. He caught himself.

Oooooh you're my hot and ready boy, aren't you?

Though he knew she meant this as endearment and permission, something in her tone alerted the last stop impulse still standing amid his wilted willpower. Uh ... I don't know.

Don't know?

He receded as much as the confined space would allow. Um. This is nice but ...

Huh?

Oh. I don't know.

What don't you know?

What I'm doing. Mostly.

What we're doing.

Yeah I guess.

We're having fun in a sleeping bag.

I'll say. Most fun I've ever had.

Wait a minute ... Aldis rolled to her side. He could see in the moonlight that she was propping her head on a crooked elbow and regarding him with wide-eyed intent. You've done this before. Right?

Nope.

A virgin? Wouldn't you know it. I mean how old are you?

Almost sixteen.

Her physical pull-back nearly alarmed him. If they had not been bound by the confines of the truck bed she might have gotten completely away from touch. A thing he now knew he never wanted to happen.

Holy ... I know you look young and cute. But ... How are you driving this truck if you're underage?

I'm pretty good at it.

But still.

It's a long story.

Wow. Gee. I guess I'm robbing the cradle.

Hope you don't mind.

As long as you don't. Being in bed with an older woman. Aldis nearly chuckled. Of seventeen.

I like it. I like it a lot.

Oh you are so sweet. You know how when you meet someone? And you know there's something special?

I didn't know before but I think I do now.

You are so sweet.

Though he understood that the content of their talk was truly vapid he also knew he needed this pause in the corporeal action to consider a sober next move. I sure didn't think this would happen.

Well ... nothing has actually happened. Yet.

That's what I'm thinking about. Or trying to.

That's so considerate. Are you sure you're only fifteen?

The way I feel now I'm not sure of anything. Would it be okay if we just talked a bit?

Most boys in sleeping bags with girls don't talk much.

I guess. I can see why.

But it's sweet though. That you want to talk. Do you mind if we touch too?

Mind? I like it a lot. I like it too much.

Don't be scared. I'm not going to bite. Unless you want me to. And I'm on the pill so …

Oh. Well. That's important too I guess.

Important? Hee hee … not a word I would expect to hear while making out with a cute guy in the back of a pickup truck. But whatever. Are you going to slip out of these underwear? She reached into them and gripped him fullhand. Or do you want me to do it for you?

Uh … I'd better not. We'd. We better not.

You are so ready …

I know. But.

… And so am I.

I can't.

Aldis unhanded him. You do like me, don't you? She leaned and kissed him so gently that the slightness of contact and the pure intimacy of it nudged him toward panic.

I sure do. That's why.

Thereupon began their heartfelt dialogue in the star-filled open languid night. Whilst intoxicated equal parts by excitement and fatigue, Robin nevertheless managed to contribute half the conversation. Both he and she manoeuvred conjoined legs and arms so as to cool sufficiently the ongoing heat of their closeness and the internal generation of a near-palpable emotional electricity.

Eventually they slept. Out of sight below the rise the drone of trucks on the open highway was just distant enough to be soothing.

Robin had been unaware of losing consciousness so he lurched in utter surprise to be wakened by full sunlight to the face and commotion roundabout. There were voices and movement audible but not to be seen over the sides of the box. Though eager to stir he was reluctant to disturb the perfect spoon configuration of the sleep posture he held with Aldis.

She sighed and stretched, then turned to him smiling. Morning, sunshine.

Oh man … did we fall asleep?

We sure did.

Are you okay … is it … okay for you to be here?

I told you last night, Robin. I'm my own person.

I remember. Then I fell asleep I guess.

You were gone gone gone. I guess you have pretty long days huh.

Yeah. Guess this one's got to start soon too.

Unfortunately yes.

They went about donning clothes. Robin judged the time to be sometime around eight, a late hour relative to that he had been accustomed to on the road. The smell of food came from the same source as last night's lentils and immediately put him in mind of the breakfast that had been mentioned. Then he remembered the repair job he'd volunteered for and rued that the moments presently would not endure.

As Aldis jumped down from the truck with her billowing dress and bandana accessory fully arranged he remembered everything and gladness inflated his chest and a rush of something he had not known before pumped to his head. He neared, put his arms around her, and did not let go for a full minute. They swayed together in the morning brightness.

Oooh you are so sweet.

I just had to do this.

Yes you did.

Yes I did.

You are so sweet. Aldis hugged harder. Are there any more of you?

His embrace lost its energy. Huh?

Did they make just one of you? Got a brother or two hidden away?

He stayed locked to her. Um. I think I'm the only one that's exactly like me.

Oh well.

As he'd seldom been bashful in his life he could not identify the reason for the heat in his face. Remembering there were other things to do this fine day he swung open the door of the truck to retrieve his tools. Oh. Do you want a drink of this? Karen left it last night.

Aldis's eyes narrowed. Orange Crush?

Yeah. Said it was her last.

Oh yeah? Aldis took the bottle and easily thumbed the cap twiddling off into the bushes. See this? The top has been opened.

I wondered about that. What did she do?

She spiked it is what she did. That bitch.

Why?

You didn't drink any of it, did you?

No.

She's got some killer acid. Been turning people on whether they liked it or not all across the country.

Oh.

I saw her stash. She's got like five hundred hits of window-pane that she sells to get us across the country. Aldis poured the amber fluid onto the ground. This is like really wicked of her. I'm so sorry.

Why are you guys travelling together?

She's my cousin. I mean she's cool but sometimes she's not, you know? I think she's jealous that I like you. She's actually jealous of everybody most of the time.

Well. I wish you were going my way.

We talked about that last night. I hope you remember. Me and her have got some people we need to see at Expo.

Such a long way.

It's a long way everywhere and sometimes it isn't. That's just how it is.

I guess.

Look at you. Mister I'm-only-fifteen-and-driving-this-truck-to-Vancouver Island!

Ha ha.

She stepped to him and two-handedly held his forehead to hers. Victoria. The end of October. Okay?

Huh?

I'll meet you. She kissed him.

Oh. Sure.

You be there.

The end of October. Victoria. I can't hardly wait.

She kissed him again and passed him a piece of paper. Here's the number. Call me.

For sure.

As they broke it up one more time Robin spotted Percival stepping out of a semi-trailer cab out by the roadway with a brown paper wrapping in his hand.

He savoured a last look at smiling Aldis as she strode away waving, then gripped the tool box and made for the VW. A queue of fellow roadway denizens were waiting there with dish and bowl in hand for what he now saw was a hearty porridge being issued from the side door. He and Percival stood and ate a breakfast bowl of cooked grain that looked to him like the stuff he'd been harvesting these past seasons in the fields he had left behind and that he knew not if he would ever see again. When the porridge was gone the work began.

Using two jacks and as many wood blocks as could be gathered they raised the front end sufficient for both of them to slide under. They removed the leaking master brake cylinder. This was the kind of work Robin was used to on larger and more accessible rolling stock but he managed to pull the connecting wires and hydraulic line without damage. Percival was ready with a bucket when the trickle of fluid issued from the brake lines. They fitted the new part into the threaded port, replenished the fluid, and reattached the wires in short enough time.

Percival started the van and pumped the brakes. Hey. Right up again. Nice work.

Good.

Thanks for the help. Can't wait to get back on the road.

Me neither. Before the cops come anyway.

Yeah … I guess you don't want to run into them especially.

Not especially.

You're on the young side of legal driving I guess.

You guess right.

Well you sure know your way around mechanical stuff. Can't thank you enough.

I appreciate breakfast.

Any time, man.

Robin had his tools collected and closed the kit. See ya.

Yup. For sure.

Luck.

Back atcha.

They shook hands.

• • •

Robin pulled the '42 out of camp as the sun was noticeably heating the dust, vehicles, and people still hanging about. He waved to the phalanx of lanky, long haired, tie-dyed personages waiting by the highway. He did not try to see if Aldis was there among them in the bunch headed toward the Trans-Canada but he knew she might be or perhaps had already caught the good ride and was on her way. His thoughts of her were perfect. His hands felt better on the steering wheel and the motor's growl was more satisfying than it had ever been. The breeze through the side window refreshed him tooling north on the main road for a mile or so before turning left to proceed once again across open range.

By the map Orville had given him it seemed that save for crossing a major artery or two he would by this route avoid civilization most of the way to the Rockies. The day thus passed in the usual manner. He was now expert at negotiating the faint tracks that indicated the way and deep draws and shallow currents and cattle herds that impeded it. At times Robin needed extra caution as the tracks sometimes slanted so far as to threaten rollover.

The land began to be not completely concerned with agriculture. As the undulant relief stretched out he noted at first a few and then many pumpjacks pecking petro-fluid from the stubbled earth.

By mid-afternoon he could see the great granite curtain of the mountains and oil extraction machines bobbed up and down as far as Robin could make out across the countryside. The land was dry, grass crunched underfoot. By late afternoon he was within sight of a large town which he judged to be Cardston. Sensing that another accumulation of hitchhikers and others of the type with whom he'd spent last night might be nearby he sought a likely location.

The highway appeared as dusk thickened. He flicked on his headlights and had not travelled far on blacktop when he glanced a pair of vehicles and a tent to one side. He swung off the road and in minutes had been invited to sit by a fire. There was no food so he shared what was left in the cooler that was now not at all cool so it was just as well that the little crowd whomped up the last of it. There was some music but not much. There was no one like Aldis.

He took this thought to his bedroll and slept a solid night without interruption. Early sun broke through low cloud and lit the nearby snow-peaks with a declarative glow. As he stood to receive this visual gift he understood that he was now looking at the leading edge of the province of British Columbia. A sentiment of having come far impacted his heart. Then an urge to continue seized him headlong. But searching the map in the dawn light he saw now that open range and farmland and viable off-main routes were become scarce if not nonexistent.

He was approached by a long-braided middle-aged woman bearing a tray of odd crockery. Good morning, young traveller.

Morning, ma'am.

Would you like some tea? She held forth the tray so that Robin could see that the rough cups and saucers held a steaming amber liquid.

Okay. I guess. I'm more used to coffee but …

I won't be offended if you don't like it.

Robin took a cup and carefully sipped. Hmmm. Well. It's not coffee but it's not bad.

My own blend. Perfect for the road. Amaranthine tea.

Amar … anthie?

Tea for the ages. Ageless tea. Everlasting tea.

Well. He took in a full mouthful and began to find an enjoyment in its fullness.

Take a biscuit.

Robin two-fingered a thick, shortbread-looking cookie from the tray. I sure am grateful for the bite. Ran out of food yesterday.

They stood for a time sipping tea and munching.

Robin accepted the offer of another biscuit. Out on the highway they could observe that a few of the camp-dwellers had begun the day's hitchhike troll in either direction. He handed back cup and saucer. Thanks a lot for that. Grateful as heck.

You are welcome and best of luck for your journey.

Uh ... hey. An idea struck. Uh. About that. Do you know anybody who's heading west? He motioned to the phalanx of expectant hitchhikers.

West. Hmmm. Almost everybody is going north to the big highway. But ... He followed her on a slow stroll back to what he assumed was her vehicle. She gently pushed down the trunk lid of a well-maintained Nash Metropolitan. I'll ask around. Are you leaving soon?

Soon as possible.

He returned to the '42 and began its morning mechanical ablutions. The gas tank was topped and oil checked and he was shaking the coarser particles from the air filter when a lean fellow with a khaki packsack strode up. You looking for a rider?

Actually no. A driver.

Oh.

Going west?

Yeah.

How far?

Nelson. Well Balfour actually.

Where's that?

Nearly to Nelson.

Okay. Got a driver's licence?

Yup.

Can you drive this kind of truck? It's three on the floor. Not much top-end speed but it'll make forty-five without too much trouble.

Well sure. But. Where did you come from? Why not drive it yourself?

Robin told his entire story in a pre-considered two-minute nutshell.

Wow.

So you see what I need to do.

Yeah. Well. He swung off his packsack and held it with two hands. Okay. I'm your man.

How old are you?

Eighteen. And you're like just fourteen and you drove this thing all the way over the rangeland from south Saskatchewan?

I'm fifteen, but … yeah, that's right.

Hoo-boy. This kind of wild time I just gotta get in on.

Yeah well. Having a guy who doesn't look young as me drive us through the Rockies is the way I'm trying not to have too much wild time.

I get you, man. I get you for sure. Ha ha.

Robin offered his hand. Robin.

Tim. They shook.

Aside from a tooth-loosening geargrind pulling out of the camp, Robin saw that Tim understood how to drive a no-frills farm vehicle with at least some measure of competence. They were soon motoring smooth blacktop with windows open at a hair-fluttering fifty miles per hour. It was a relative luxury to cover such ground and not even be driving but Robin did not take to it readily. He monitored Tim's treatment on the clutch and judged the steadiness of his positioning in the traffic lane. Numerous times he forced himself not to call out or even comment when his driver followed so close to a semi-trailer rig that the vehicle was vacuum-buffeted nearly to the point of fishtailing.

The mountain range shortly began to dominate the forward vista. It felt odd and weirdly intimidating to be leaving the flatlands he had grown so accustomed to. He fought to calm an increasing chest-pound anxiety. Though indifferent to casual conversation he realized it might be the only way to fight off an irrational sense of dread.

Balfour. He had to bark over the din of wind blast and engine. Is that a town?

More like just an area. District. My uncle's got a house there. So will I someday.

You're going to have a house?

Gonna build it myself. On three acres. Uncle's gonna sell it to me cheap. Gonna scrounge the lumber. Nothing fancy. More'n likely pretty rough actually but it'll be mine.

Nice.

Yeah. Better than back there I'll tell you. Tim head-gestured behind them.

What's back there?

Mormonism.

What?

My parents' religion. Didn't you see the big temple?

Where? In Cardston?

Right in the middle of town. First and largest Mormon tabernacle outside the You Ess of Eh.

I didn't pass through. Came out of the scrub.

Good for you. It's all crap. Religion. Especially LDS.

LDS?

Tim looked over with a faint smile and a new friendliness in his eyes that Robin found more welcome than he imagined he ever would. You sure don't know much, do you?

I'm learning fast as I can.

Latter-day Saints. They flatter themselves don't they though?

I'd never call myself a saint. Robin heard himself laugh out loud for the first time in weeks. Even if I was!

I'm with you there. Though to be fair, I think they're referring to the symbols they worship rather than themselves. I knew all that stuff one time. As a kid. In religious school. Forgot most of it. Glad I did. Don't care.

That's kind of where I'm at too.

Only reason I was there. Only reason I stayed too long. Was a girl. A real pretty girl.

I can relate.

Can ya? He looked away from the road and grinned at Robin.

Yup.

Well good on ya. Tim grimly resumed his careful scan of the road ahead. It's fine living out on the land in a place like Balfour. But it's trouble when you visit the folks in belief-land.

Things get awkward?

Not a strong enough word. Tense. Gets in the way of all kinds of family affections if you know what I mean.

Robin looked out over the rolling countryside and let the wind from the side window push his eyelids slowly closed. That's too bad. Family's important.

Well … yeah. I guess.

A calm stop at a busy truck diner allowed as big a lunch as both youths' limited budget would manage and a gathering of portable food from a convenience store. More miles of breeze in the window and the dull clamour of the engine creating consistency of time and movement made Robin give up fighting drowsiness and finally succumb to an unconscious drift.

He woke when Tim shouted above the noise that something was wrong.

The chill air abruptly told him that climbing had occurred. Robin saw that they were partway up one of the long hills that ascended into the Crowsnest Pass through the first rock cleft of prairies' end. Tim was steering the '42 into an observation pull-out with telescopes mounted on permanent concrete plinths and tourists standing around with cameras.

Robin only noticed the scut of blue smoke they were issuing when the truck stopped and the vapours blew their way past them on a breeze over the cliffside. Damn. Forgot to change oil this morning.

You mean it's old?

No. It's new. But we have to replace it with heavier. Robin rummaged beneath the seat and pulled out a gallon container. When the engine cooled slightly he slid under the front end to loosen the oil drain bolt. With funnel and bucket arranged accordingly he captured the fuming fluid as it gushed down. He replaced the bolt and slid back out.

Dang. Tim was inspecting the numbers on the side of the new oil. You think of everything. This is gooey stuff.

Well. It wasn't exactly me. Robin was grateful again to Orville for thinking of the requirements the truck would have surmounting the long grinding pulls of mountain driving.

They were hunched over the open cowling carefully funnelling the goopy fluid into the crankcase when a Royal Canadian Mounted Police cruiser pulled into the turnoff.

Robin touched Tim's arm. Your name is Robin Wallenco.

Huh? Tim had seen the police presence but not reacted. Why is that my name? It's your name isn't it?

It's the name on the registration.

Oh. Well he's driving on by.

Sure hope so.

Wouldn't do any good anyway. He'd ask for ID. Driver's licence.

Yeah … I'm trying to figure that out. Let's get this done and get out of here.

If you insist.

I don't insist. It's just what we have to do.

Well. You have to do it maybe. Not me.

Are you going to help me or not?

Sure but you don't have to talk to me like that.

Like what?

Like you're some kind of mastermind or something.

I'm not a mastermind or anything like it. I just want to get out of here before the cops notice us. That's all.

Well why? Don't you own this truck?

Yes.

And I'm driving it for you. Right?

Yeah.

What's the hassle then?

I just don't want to answer any questions.

It isn't stolen, is it? Is it stolen? Tim drew back from their work and wiped his hands with a rag. If it's stolen I'm like out of here, man. I already had one run-in with the law and I never want to do it again.

It's not stolen. Not exactly.

Not exactly?

I got it from a guy who didn't want it anymore. He said I could have it. He died before he could legally transfer it to me. That's all.

Whoa.

What do you mean whoa?

Sounds iffy.

What does iffy mean? For crying out loud let's get this done and get out of here.

The cruiser paused at the line of tourists peering down upon undulant foothills and cultivated dry land.

Robin furiously spun the oil cap tight. Okay let's get out of here.

Do you think that's a good idea? I mean right now? The guy is just sitting there. He might notice we're in a hurry or something.

Then drive gently out of here. Just get in.

Hey you can't talk to me like that.

Oh for crying out loud.

Why don't you just mellow down, man? You're getting obnoxious.

Robin could feel himself losing something inside. He leapt into the driver's seat and swept his hand to the ignition key. It wasn't there.

Gimme the key.

I don't think it's a good idea for you to drive, man.

I don't care what you think. Gimme my key.

No.

Hand it over. Robin jumped from the cab and lunged at the older youth.

Forget it.

The tussle involved a boy trying to reach the top reach of a larger boy and eventually devolved into a roiling mutual stumble against the truck and to the ground. Robin wrenched and struck and writhed. Tim fought to protect himself and then appeared frantic in a moment when he realized by Robin's vehemence he might be fighting for his life.

Stop fooling around!

Gimme the damn key!

You're not gonna get it ...

They rolled together until both were startled by the shine of brown leather boots in their mutual sightline. The constable stood over them.

Am I going to have to tell you guys to break it up?

The boys scrambled upward, brushing themselves of the road dust and assuming their best non-criminal facial expressions.

The policeman's next query came through an amused chuckle. Now what the heck is the big idea here? Though the man was smiling and young — not too many years past the median age of the combatants — his tone was serious enough.

Nothing.

Nothing.

Well ... heh heh. I'm not sure what's worse. You fellows fighting about something or you fellows fighting about nothing.

The odd texture of this remark stalled the boys from any kind of response.

I guess I'm not going to get a bright answer from either of you two at that. You're not even that good of fighters. Unevenly matched for one thing. The constable turned to Tim. Why are you the big guy picking on this smaller guy?

These words — accompanied by appropriate pointings of a finger — penetrated the minds but again did not elicit spoken answers from either subject.

Okay never mind. What are your names?

Tim.

Dave.

I'll assume you've never been asked for identification by police. The chuckle was gone and the smile faded. You're going to have to supply me a full name each. That is not just a first name but also a surname. And especially not just a contraction of a first name. Not a nickname either. A full name. Remember that.

Yes, sir.

Okay then. Names?

Timothy Waters.

David Mellor.

That's better. And who owns this truck? Or did you guys just happen to fall against it during your big-time set-to here a minute ago?

Uhh ... Robin tried to think and found he could not.

It's broken down. Tim shifted and spoke at the same time. The guy who owns it's name is Rob something. We don't know his last name. Tim pointed to the road and beyond the horizon. He's hitchhiking down there to get some parts.

Oh. Rob you say. It's broken down, is it? What's the problem?

Don't know myself. It just started smoking hard up this last hill here and he figured it was something.

Something, eh? We're back to that.

Rob asked us to stay here and look after it.

You were riding with him?

Yup.

And he's hitching back down the road?

Yup.

Well I just came up the road. Didn't see anybody hitching. He got a ride right away. Trucker.

A trucker, eh? Hmmm. Does your friend here talk?

Yes, sir.

Dave, is it? Is that right what Tim here says? The truck is Rob's. He's gone to get parts.

Yes, sir.

Well it's certainly a fine truck. Oldie but a goodie. I hope things work out.

Yes, sir.

You tell Rob he'll have to have it towed if it won't run anymore. I'll be back around by nightfall. If it's still here I'll have to have it removed at his expense.

Yes, sir.

And stop fighting, okay?

Okay.

Okay.

You seem like friends anyway. What was it about?

Oh … I forget.

Me too.

See, fellows? It's never worth getting punchy. Whatever it is. Always go the diplomacy route, okay?

Okay.

Good.

The constable strode to the rear of the '42. Fine old beastie. He pulled a notepad and peered at the licence plate. All the way from Saskabush … He noted something on the pad then looked up and walked slowly the rest of the way around the truck to face the boys. Now given that this Rob fellow left you guys in charge I guess it's you I ask to see the registration. Would that be okay?

Uh sure. I don't know where he keeps it.

Well most people use the glove compartment. Does this old-timer have one of those?

Robin moved to the passenger side and reached through the open window. Here it is. He handed the paper to the constable.

Thanks … A long look at both sides of the government document and more notations in the notebook and then an audible closing of same. Well for your information boys your driver's name is Robin. But I'm sure you can just call him Rob.

Last name's Wallenco if you're interested. He handed the paper back to Robin.

Both boys nodded.

And by the way. You don't mind if I ask to see some identification for you fellows do you?

Uh … Tim pulled a wallet from a back pocket.

Robin stood staring at the Mountie.

Tim handed a card over and after a quick look the constable handed it back.

So Dave … The Mountie's eyes trained upon Robin. I suppose you're a little young to be carrying ID like your friend Tim here.

I don't have any.

Yeah I figured so. He nodded a gesture toward the nearby open road and looked around at the variety of tourists and sundry travellers thereabout. A lot of youth out hitting the road. Especially this summer. That what you guys are doing?

Mutual nods.

Well. Have a fine time. But look out for stuff okay? You never know about the rides you take. You never know about the drivers. Make sure Rob doesn't drink while he's whisking you off into the sunset any time okay? I've already seen too much blood on the roadway and I'm kinda new at this myself.

No sir.

Yes. For sure.

The boys stood as casual as they imagined casual would be under the strained circumstance of tourists giving them the wary eye and the Mountie imparting a solemn sermon. Then the constable put away his notepad and stepped toward the cruiser. Be sure to make Mister Robin Wallenco aware about the overnight parking situation here.

We will.

Sorry I can't be of further assistance. He nodded westward up the hill. Got to go patrol up the road.

When the cruiser was full out of sight and the tourist interest in them had ebbed, Robin and Tim turned to gaze at each other's feet.

Robin looked up first. Good work, Tim. That was some quick thinking.

Thanks … Dave … You're welcome.

Ha ha.

Where did that name come from?

I dunno. Maybe I seen it in a newspaper or something.

Got any others?

Nope.

Well it seemed to work anyway.

I don't know how we got through that.

Sometimes lying is the only way.

Damn. You might be right.

We'll see.

Where is the key?

In my pocket.

I think we should get out of here.

In a few minutes. Let the cop totally disappear.

Do you think he's gone for sure?

No telling. I doubt he bought that whole story.

Maybe we should hide out a little up the road. Just in case.

Might be a good idea.

They stood for many minutes waiting for the range of sightseers and stopped travellers, car dwellers and truck drivers to change from those who'd witnessed their tussle and the resulting police interest into those who simply saw them as a couple of young men standing by an old truck. Then they slid into respective sides, started up, and rolled away.

The Last Boy on Earth

THOUGH LIKELY THE DRIVER COULD NOT, ROBIN IN THE passenger seat detected the more sombre engine note the heavier oil facilitated and sensed with approval that they would likely now have little trouble scaling the long ascents of the Crowsnest Pass. Tim wheeled the '42 around some small lakes until a park turnoff promised swim areas and secluded trails. They pulled into a treed siding off the highway and then along a side road to secrete themselves. With feet dangling off the tailgate, admiring the view of a tree-hemmed lake, they ate sandwiches and drank colas. The mountains imposed a terrible mental confinement to prairie-oriented Robin but he knew he would get used to it. The feeling of escape — from where he had been to where he was going — and the more recent near miss with the roving RCMP carried a particular exhilaration.

So. What do you think would have happened if they'd found out you sort-of own this thing and you're only fifteen?

I don't know. Guess they'd confiscate it. Probably grab me as an underage runaway and try to get me back to my parents.

Where are your parents?

Mom's in Qualicum Beach. I don't exactly know where Dad is. I'm hoping Mom knows.

So the cops would be doing you a favour, sort of. I mean, you're going back to them anyway.

Well sure. But I want to bring this truck with me.

Yeah I get that. Weird.

It's not so weird.

I've heard of guys getting attached to their stuff. Materialism.

Material ... what?

When you get attached to things more than people. When you want more more more and don't care about anything else.

I'm not like that.

Maybe not full-on. But watch it.

I just like this truck. It's the first one I ever drove. I put a lot of work into it and did a lot of work with it.

Even so. You won't see me getting all possessive of anything. I like freedom. Freedom is carrying all you need in life on your back.

Freedom for me is where this truck can get me.

Ha ha. Well. I guess we have to leave that argument where it is. What are you gonna do after we get to where I'm going?

Just keep on.

That'll be hard. There's only one road anywhere mostly and the cops are sure to see you on it.

I'll think of something.

How much gas you got?

Robin reached back to sound knuckles on the pump tank. I guess another tank or two.

So you're gonna have to start buying gas like everybody else.

I guess.

Got money?

Some.

You'll need more than that.

They both chuckled.

You want to stay a while in Balfour? I know a way you can make some good cash.

Yeah?

My uncle has a dope farm back up in the woods.

A dope farm?

Marijuana.

I know that. But the way you said it sounded like he's growing dummies. Guys who don't know anything. Dopes.

Hardy har har ... It's a serious business around there. Most of the economy, they say. That's why I'm going back. It's drying time.

I heard that country song. Well it's drying time again. Yer gonna leave me ...

Can you get serious about anything?

Sorry. I guess I'm still kind of nervy about that cop back there. Need some yucks to loosen up.

Maybe you should pop a pill or something.

A pill? What kind of pill?

Well there's ones that calm you down. Others that jazz you up.

Sounds like weirdness to me.

It is weird that's for sure. I've known pill jockeys. It isn't pretty.

I'd never want to depend on drugs.

Well. There are worse things. You could be a boozer. Like my uncle.

Naw. Drinking doesn't appeal to me either. The little I've done of it. So far.

Ever smoke weed?

Nope.

Dropped acid?

No but almost. The other night as a matter of fact.

For real?

As near as I can figure. Some girl tried to trick me into taking it.

I did it once. Nearly freaked. It was only good at first and at the tail end.

I'm flat-out scared of it.

You? Scared?

Robin drank off the remains of his soft drink and tucked the bottle into the garbage bag that had been burgeoning the past few days in the truck bed. Don't tell anybody. Okay?

I was kidding. Of course you get scared. Everybody does.

Know what scares me most?

No. What?

The way you grind those gears from third to second.

Aw, c'mon. This old heap's got transmission problems.

Just kidding.

But on their travel resumption Robin noted Tim's greater care in tending the stick shift and also the gentle relation between revs and double-clutch. He never heard a clash of crankteeth again.

Their progress overland ended not with darkness that night but with Tim's fatigue and they pulled into an auto court outside Creston with a blinking neon "Vacancy" sign. Tim approached the office where the sign was about to be turned dark by the aging gentleman running the place.

Is there a room we could have?

The old fellow eyed the youth and then Robin, sitting in the '42. Is that there your little brother travelling with you?

Uh ... yeah.

Fine vehicle. Had one myself one time. Or one like it.

It's old but it goes.

Something like me.

Heh heh …

Just so happens I got the only room I could give you fellows. Right here by the office.

That'll be fine.

No funny stuff now.

Nope.

I'll have an eye on ya.

You're welcome to but you won't need to. We're dog-tired and just looking for a shower and a bed.

Well come along into the office here. It's eight dollars. We only take cash.

Tim motioned for Robin to come over.

It's eight bucks.

Okay. Robin dug bills out of his jeans.

The oldster looked them over under the harsh fluorescence of the small office. He pointed to Tim. How come your hair is so much longer than his?

I'm older. It's had more time to grow.

Ha.

After a shower and take-out fried chicken Robin tried to watch television. There had been none on the farm and he was only vaguely aware of an entertainment world outside his agrarian book-bound purview. He imagined that strange and wonderful things happened and social standards were being pushed. He had watched in an earlier phase of his life the first seasons of *The Beverly Hillbillies*. But as he lay out on one of the beds and peered at the motel TV he could not make sense of the scantily clad woman who lived in a bottle and had an astronaut friend. The toll of the day took him into unconsciousness before he could parse the logic of what was happening. If logic was indeed what applied.

Morning arrived ahead of schedule as the boys rolled off their respective mattresses and groaned. Robin knew the stiffness of the road would wear off when once again they were on it but he knew the wear of daily forward progress was having an overall fatiguing effect on him. A diner breakfast cheered things and the air was mountain fresh coming through the side window as they took off along the shores of a lake so giant he was not sure he'd seen a bigger one.

What's that called?

Tim glanced at the water and back to Robin before resuming his careful steer along the winding two-lane blacktop. Kootenay Lake. We gotta cross it.

Huh?

On a ferry. We catch it up ahead here.

An hour later they were in a lineup of cars waiting for the ship as it rounded a point and inched up to its berth. A surreality encroached on Robin's sense of place and time and who he was and where he was going. The sight of such an object so jarringly unexpected in this mountainous environment made him re-remember the enormity of his flight. He was far from completing this wild project and filled with a combination of wonder and dread at its risks and dangers.

He kept his turmoil covert as Tim casually rolled the '42 onto the rumbling vessel's metal deck. For now he could grasp the wild contrasts in his life and reside within them: He had a land-locked orientation, and now he had vast water beneath him. Trusting his only true possession to the drive skills of a fellow he'd been in a physical altercation with only yesterday, barrelling headlong into a confrontation with his own life with no idea what the outcome would be.

They rolled off the boat and onto a two-lane winding provincial highway following along still farther lakeside until Tim pulled the '42 off the main track and lugged up the side of a mountain. Robin saw nothing but trees. Occasionally a house would appear and then there were more trees. After a few miles of up and down but mostly up Tim turned sharp off the road onto a gravel track leading down. Then they were on a flat cleared spot where a few semi-serviceable vehicles resided beside a large house. About the building much detritus lay. Robin shortly realized that most of it was siding and trim and other things that belonged on the structure.

Welcome to Uncle Burton's place.

So this is it, is it?

Yeah. Looks like nobody's home.

Are they expecting you?

Only sort of. I mean they know I'm coming home sometime but they don't know exactly what day. Or week.

As Tim finished speaking a couple of tween-aged girls emerged from the front door and skipped to the truck.

Hey it's Cousin Tim!

Aw gee, it's good to see you guys. Tim stepped from the '42 and gripped each with a widespread arm. He turned them toward the open driver's door for a clear view of Robin.

This here's my pal Robin. He presented one slightly ahead. Robin, this is Tricia. And this is Sally.

Oooh he's cute.

Where'd you get this keen truck?

It's Robin's.

Oooh he's cute and he owns a truck.

Now don't go all crazy over him, girls. Robin's got things to do and places to go and people to see.

As Robin slipped out the passenger door he swept the key from the ignition and slipped it into the change pocket of his jeans.

Inside the cluttered multi-cat-occupied house the girls happily fabricated peanut butter and jam sandwiches for the travellers.

Tim munched ravenously. Where's your dad?

Farming.

Oh yeah. I guess he would be.

He's always farming.

There's a lot to do.

Robin looked out a wide window and noted that there were no fields about. Only trees.

Uh what kind of farming does your Uncle Burton do?

I told ya. Tim munched and spoke through peanut butter stuck teeth. Weed.

Uh-huh.

When he comes in it's best not to talk about it though.

What? Farming in general?

Anything to do with weed. People around here are touchy.

Okay.

Only if he brings it up. If he trusts you he'll more'n likely bring it up. Eventually.

All right.

After the girls had made them macaroni and cheese with sliced tomatoes on the side it was past evening when a clumping sounded on the veranda and the kitchen door opened wide in the twilight to reveal a tall man kicking off boots and stepping into the house in stockinged feet. Whose truck is that out there?

Uncle Burton.

Tim! Did you win a lottery or something?

That belongs to my new friend Robin here. Robin. Meet Burton.

A handshake. Welcome, young stranger.

Thanks.

Where you from?

Well Saskatchewan right now. Later on I'm not sure.

Sounds like a typical traveller of the times. Burton turned to look hard at his nephew. And where was Tim all these weeks?

Down in Cardston.

Cardston. That dry hole. What for?

Trying to make sense of Mom and Dad.

We all gave up on that years ago. What the hell was the point? There's work around here, you know.

Sorry, Uncle.

Sorry isn't good enough.

It was a girl. I was trying to get close to a girl if you really want to know.

Aha. Now we hear. Burton comic-mimed a search of the kitchen and mugged a quizzical look. Well, where is she?

Not here, that's for sure.

You struck out with her?

Oh she liked me fine enough but apparently I'm not Mormon enough for her.

Ha. You're not Mormon at all. Did she not know that going in?

She tried to convert me back.

She did, did she.

It didn't take.

Ha ha ha … Burton collected both Tim and Robin in an assembled hug and gave each hearty back slaps. Never give up boys. Never give up. Burton sat and leaned across the kitchen table as the girls scampered out of sight. And how is my religious nutcase brother and family? Still no good for nothing but praying, I'll bet.

They treat me fine.

Christian charity.

It's pretty white-bread all right. All that church-going. Boring as all hell but … I guess they see something in it.

Oh you best not try to penetrate the great mysteries of LDS devotion. They'll kidnap you one of these days. Inject you with their religious toxin. Make you into a cloth-man for sure. Pious to a fault. Preachy to the point of pedantic inanity.

You know I don't cotton to that stuff at all.

Good boy. Burton snorted and looked away and back again. Are you ready to work?

Yeah.

It's about time. I've been all alone in the drying and wondering if I'd ever get finished.

Well I'm here now.

Burton stood and motioned for them to follow him into a dim living room. Once there he plopped heavily into a worn vinyl lounger. The place was lit by one low-wattage table lamp. Sit down, fellows. Make yourselves at home. Tricia!

The girl appeared immediately at the kitchen doorway. Yes, Daddy.

Get us some beers!

Yes, Daddy.

Robin found a perch amid felines and refuse on an antique divan only slightly less filthy and animal-soiled than the rest of the fetid room. When the bottles were distributed he took his and held it to forehead for the benefit of its moist coolness, which at that moment granted him a strange comfort.

So Robin. Are you keen to make a little cash?

I'm not sure.

Oh? What are you sure of?

Not much other than I'm heading west as fast as I can.

But surely you can stand a little income to put into that gas tank.

Maybe.

My young friend … Burton took a swig. Do you know anything about marijuana farming?

Nope. Not a thing.

Well that's okay. You're a little on the raw side of it age-wise anyway. I wouldn't have expected you'd smoked the stuff very long at all.

I don't use it. Never have. Not sure I ever will.

Ha! Burton took another healthy pull on his beer bottle and turned to Tim. Hear that? What would this country come to if everybody thought like our Robin here?

Each to his own I guess. Tim sipped lightly at his bottle.

He's a pillar of society, I tell you. A stalwart. He's the guy we build our stoned nirvana around. The last sober man. There will have to be one last one, you know.

If you say so.

Without further words Burton pulled a lighter from a pocket and a hand-rolled cigarette from another and inserted it between lips to put it to fire. He drew deep and handed the joint off to Tim's waiting hand. Burton looked Robin's way and chuckled. He drank the last of his beer in two gulps and dropped the empty onto the floor. Almost instantly one of the girls was back in the room with a fresh one.

Thank you, sweetie … Burton accepted the bottle and pressed himself farther into his chair. But could you bring me the whisky?

Burton took the joint back from Tim and regarded Robin through twisting smoke that fouled the light of the lamp and drifted to a permanent smog in the room. He wielded the fuming stick in his hand. So you don't know anything about growing dope.

No, sir.

I take it by earlier conversation that you're a farmer
nonetheless?

On dry land. Wheat and barley mostly.

So no inkling about our business here?

Well. It's a plant you grow, I guess. I've grown lots of plants.

It's more complicated than that. Lots more.

Tricia arrived with a full bottle of Canadian Club and three
glasses. She carefully placed everything on the coffee table.

Burton gestured to the display. Even more than making this
fine distilled product I would say.

Oh.

That's right. Mostly because of its ... non-legality ... you
have to do everything yourself. Let me give you a little run-
down. He unscrewed the bottle and poured a large shot of liquor without offering any to the boys. First of all you have to
take the plant out of the ground, roots and all.

Burton took a long drink, then puffed hard on the dope and
sighed heavily. That's a backbreaker all by itself. Then you haul
it all into a dark room with no light for a day or so and then
you're cutting off roots and removing all the larger leaves. Every
plant has like about one hundred to one hundred fifty of them.
Then you hang buds and stalks in a dark dry temperature-
controlled room for five days or so. You've got to make sure the
air is moving so there's sufficient ventilation etcetera etcetera.
You check all the time that they're drying and not rotting. All
the time watching for mould and insects and fungi and a host
of other possible antagonisms.

When it's all dry you and hopefully your crew ... Burton
grimaced toward Tim between heavy gulps of his drink. You
and hopefully your crew start the pruning. You take out the
main stock but not all the stock. And so forth. You have little
branches anywhere from four to fourteen inches long to put

into a container with a tight lid overnight. Then prune the buds and take all the small leaves out close to the bud.

This is killer labour. I've seen guys go cross-eyed doing this all day. So then you have to store the whole crop back in the containers and hang around for a couple of intense days putting on and taking off the lids of the containers every eight hours or so.

After all that the stuff is finally ready to smoke.

Burton poured a long refill. If you know much about growing areas you'll wonder what we're doing here on a mountainside instead of down in a gulley somewhere where most people usually grow it. Well. Right around you here is my place that used to be good for berries and even grapes. If there was a wine industry I might be in business but there's only talk of it so far. So I grow the stuff on the mountainside I have that gets a particular amount of sunshine and has a natural spring for irrigation. It couldn't be better conditions and makes the product unique.

Burton put away his second glass of whisky in a single deep draught. Thereupon he launched into a further wide-ranging tutorial concerning the vagaries of illicit horticultural endeavours. The wordflow became a steadier current the more time passed. Robin noted that the whisky bottle was getting near half-empty.

So Robin. What do you think of all that?

Sounds like a lot of work.

It sure as hell is. Burton waveringly poured himself a slightly smaller whisky and sipped it with a scowl. He gazed quizzically at the sputtered marijuana joint still in his fingers.

It occurred to Robin that the man was emulating — even down to the after-gulp grimace — the hard-drinking movie tough guys he remembered watching on TV.

I'm glad you have an appreciation, kid. I have three acres growing at any one time. Right now I've got over a ton that's just dried out and ready to process.

Wow.

Damn right wow. Burton burped loudly and long. You can — *braaaap* — say that again for sure.

Jeez, Uncle Burton. What's with the burp show?

Aw damn it, Tim ... Burton hit his midsection with a rounded fist several times as if trying to dislodge further gas. Happens whenever I mix beer and moonshine.

Ha ha.

Burton sat back with empty glass in hand and gestured to the dwindling booze supply. You boys help yourselves.

Tim leaned over and poured himself a modest ounce. Robin did not move but sipped slow at the warming beer in his hand. Burton regarded him with watery eyes.

I take it you're gonna not partake.

I'm kind of new to hard stuff. This beer's fine.

You know what Humphrey Bogart once said. About drinking.

No I don't.

Well I transpose it to all the wonderful intoxicants and hallucinogens nature has to offer human consciousness ... Burton interrupted his lesson to take a fruitless drag on the dead joint. He gazed quizzically at the cold ash in his fingers and tossed it aside. For a pregnant second he stared darkly at his captive student. He said I don't trust anybody who doesn't drink.

He did, did he.

Look it up.

I might some day, sir.

Ha. You're a respectful one, aren't you?

I try.

Ah I can tell you're a good boy, Robin. You're a good and fine boy, aren't ya? Anybody ever tell you that?

Some maybe. At times.

Ha ha ... Where'd you find this fine young lad, Timmy? He's a source of fascination to me.

We met on the road, Uncle. Outside Pincher Creek. He needed me to drive his truck for him.

Aha ... I wondered at your age. And proudly the owner shall we say of that particular exhibit outside.

I do own it.

Oh I'm not challenging that fact, my friend. Only confirming that there is a legal registration of said vehicle. There is, isn't there? I have a professional interest.

Everything seems to be okay, Uncle. We came through a scrape with a ruckmump near Frank Slide and Robin was cool as a butternut squash.

Aha. I knew we had a calm customer here by the way he just sits there listening. By the way he drinks little and talks less. The way his eyes survey the room and the people in it. He's wary! You're living on the edge in some way shape or form aren't you now, good Robin?

I guess you could say.

That's right, m'lad. Keep it up. Play your cards close to your face. Play them in your mind only. Tell no one what your hand is. Keep your secrets. In fact that is the essence of our success here. No one discusses any business but their own and only with their own. You will find our people open to a point and then closed to a fault. It's the only way to run life on these great hemp hillsides.

I'll remember your advice, sir.

It'll be a lesson well learned. Burton leaned forward to pour another careful drink and simultaneously fix his young

interlocutor with as somber a stare as might be managed with
the load of intoxicants now in him. Now Robin. Let me ask
you a simple question.

Okay.

Notwithstanding what my dear nephew has earlier in-
formed us of. Are you. In any way. Connected. With any kind
of cop. Or law enforcement outfit or some kind of family relationship with one sort of police agency or other? I mean …
Burton leaned so far ahead as he spoke that his perch on the
chair became tenuous. I have good reason to ask, having taken
the risk of telling you all this. You understand what we are
doing here?

No.

No you don't understand? Or no you have no cop
connections?

No, there's no police in my family.

Good. Glad to hear it. Burton sat back. We can do business.

We can?

Sure we can. You want to earn some coin, don't you?

Well I —

And you are the owner of that fine and orderly looking
pickup truck out there, aren't you?

Yes.

Well that brings me to our problem around here. Did you
see my vehicles?

Yes.

Not so good. Are they?

I'd say not.

You're an astute judge of rolling machinery, my fine sir.
No. I have no rustbuckets running at all right now. Neither do
I have at present any community connection with a truck and
driver since my last one got tagged in Castlegar last week …

What? Tim jolted in his seat. Trevor got busted? How did that happen?

Burton waved a hand at his nephew without taking his eyes off Robin. Never mind. He'll be okay. Just not available right now.

Well, jeez!

So Robin. I have a thousand-pound delivery deadline falling on me tomorrow and your presence here as a companion to my most special nephew is like some kind of divine dope-dealer intervention. No?

Uh …

Now before you say anything, I can assure you. There's minimum risk involved.

Uh.

You don't even have to cross the border. The guy has that part all lined up. Although if you would there'd be considerable extra money in it for you. But I just need it trucked down past Rossland. And it doesn't even have to be you. In fact I'd prefer that my good nephew here makes the trip. You can stay and entertain these enticing young girls. I'm sure you've noticed their flouncing about the premises.

I'm headed west.

And all I'm asking — with an offer of fine compensation — is that you or more to the point your pickup head south for a bit.

If you don't mind I can't do it. And I wouldn't ever let it out of my sight either. Even though I know Tim is a good driver.

Are you sure?

I'm sorry but. No.

Burton drew a long breath and finished the whisky in his glass. He shifted in his chair and faced Tim. He says no.

I heard.

Like he thinks he has a choice.

Uncle Burt. Don't get like that.

Don't get like what? You don't know anything about like what I'll get. If I choose to.

Robin's got the right to say no. We'll find a way to get that dope down to the border.

That's not the point. Burton cleared a spot before him on the table and fumbled at a small cedar box. He sprinkled out a mound of white power and looked to his two companions. Anyone?

Nope. Tim drank from his beer. Not for me.

Robin said nothing.

Well … Burton took a short plastic straw from a shirt pocket and in two audible sessions sucked the powder up into both nostrils. Ahhhh! His smile was twisted.

Robin's apprehensions rose high into his chest.

Burton rummaged the table for another joint to light up. He found one among the paraphernalia near the almost-empty whisky bottle. The point is … He slipped the stick between his lips and lit the end. The point is. Burton spoke with smoke coming from every orifice of his face. What I say goes around here. That's the point.

But Burt … Tim's entreaty was interrupted by his uncle's forceful flinging of the flaming joint into Tim's face. It struck his forehead, sending a starburst to his eyes.

While Tim bolted up slapping at marijuana embers Burton gripped a length of wood that had been leaning against his chair. Robin had earlier surmised it was for poking at the cats. He now decided it was meant for much more serious use.

Burton blearily turned toward Robin. What kind of fella are you … one who runs from the fire? Or one who runs toward it?

Without further words Burton stood unsteadily to swing the club and strike the side of eye-rubbing Tim's head. The youth staggered and nearly fell. Robin sprang out of his chair to move as much aside and away from the action as he could. He stood for a moment surveying; the only escape was past the swinging menace.

Burton swung the stick indiscriminately and stepped aside the cluttered ottoman and nearly toppled as his foot fouled in the detritus there. Robin knew it was a matter of short instants before he would be physically set upon by the lumbering drunkard. Then Tim lunged and he and Burton descended to a writhing mishmash atop the coffee table and then to the floor. Musk and grime rose visibly into the disturbed air. Through the melee Robin could see that Tim had seized the older man and with a closed fist hammered him about the face while avoiding the weakening swing of the stick.

That's how I got caught! Slam. Going along with one of your little jobs. Slam. You're not gonna do it to me again. Slam. And you're not gonna do it to anybody else neither. Slam.

Burton seemed to wake from the battering and respond sluggishly to his nephew's condemnations both physical and verbal. I don't have to be forgiven for all the things I've done … His mewling tone struck an odd feeling in Robin even as he measured the greater import of picking the right moment to perform a running overleap of the combatants.

There was no sign of the girls as he ran through the kitchen and out through the dark to the '42. He dug the key from his jeans and got the engine started. As he pulled on the headlights Tim fell panting against the driver's door, his face close to Robin through the open window. Good. Get going. It's the best way.

Are you okay?

I'll be fine. He's unconscious.

In the fractured light Robin saw blood at Tim's temple and his eyes were red to the point of appearing to bleed. Are you sure?

It's okay, it's okay. There was anger in Tim's insistence. Just get out of here. Take a right at the main road. Drive over the bridge and through town. This time of night you shouldn't have trouble. Then go all the way 'til you're past Winlaw. Get off the road by morning wherever you are. Take the service route over the mountain toward Fauquier. You can drive that by day. Nobody goes there. It's rough but you can make it. After that I don't know what you're gonna do.

Okay. Gee, thanks. You sure you don't want to come along?

It's okay. He'll sober up.

Jeez.

You better get going.

I guess.

Tim held a hand out for shaking. It was fun. I'll look for you out on the coast.

Do that.

As there were no lights in the driveway and the switchback ascending to the roadway came quickly Robin could not make out his friend in the rear-view. It was only after a half hour running on the lonely highway that he began to breathe normally. The novelty of driving at night only descended once the shock of what he had seen wore partially away.

There was little traffic in either direction and he knew that all cars coming and following would not be able to discern the age or almost anything about other drivers on the road. This certainty wore thin as he crossed the well-lit bridge over the west arm of Kootenay Lake and entered the city heart of Nelson. It was a first for him to execute the routine aspects of urban driving. There were traffic lights to obey. Lanes to precisely travel within. Pedestrians to look out for. Streetlights flashed alternately overhead as he prowled with whitened knuckles across the city.

So careful was he in motoring correctly that he nearly missed the turnoff for the direction he'd been advised to take. He nevertheless connected with the westward lakeside forested route and drove and drove for what seemed too far. He recalled mention of a place called Winlaw and in his lights finally saw a sign for the place.

He was beginning to like night travel, saw its potential in getting him where he needed to go, and almost rued turning off the road into a parking lot back of a closed gas and convenience store. He parked at the rear and switched off. By the dome light his watch indicated 1:14 a.m. He got out and looked around by the single lamp that burned dimly over the fuel island and was satisfied that any road traffic could not see the '42 where it stood and that he could safely spend the night here. As he pulled his sleeping bag out of the box and re-entered the cab, large raindrops began to fall. By the time he curled onto the seat with covers wrapped around him the drumming upon the roof was a soothing tattoo that sent him into dreamless sleep.

• • •

With dawn and vehicles moving about and doors opening and closing Robin woke into an accustomed hunger. He peered above the dashboard to see that a few other vehicles had entered the rain-washed area but seemed unoccupied. Then he noted that the place included a diner. The back entrance was open and swinging to allow breakfast seekers to enter directly from the parking lot. He made for the door.

A use of the washroom perhaps more elaborate than the average traveller — he was becoming adept at the ninety-second under-clothes paper-towel bath — and a plate of ham and eggs with an extra side of hash browns set him up perfectly to contemplate the events of the previous night. After a careful weighing of all that had transpired and all that he thought had transpired he was no closer to understanding the dynamics. He could only conclude that Tim's family were beyond companionability. By the time he'd gulped the last of his fourth cup of coffee he'd dismissed the incident as something he could do nothing about and that in the span of a person's life might mean little or nothing.

In the convenience store he gathered a range of packaged snacks and chocolate bars with several cans of lemonade and iced tea. He also bought a detailed map of routes — including secondary and lesser tracks — all the way to the coast. Though complicated by mountains and rivers and lakes he knew where he had to go after this. He pulled the '42 up to one of the gas pumps and for the first time in his life sat in the cab and dug out bills to cover the fill-up someone else completed for him. The gas jockey was near exactly his age and showed no hesitation. But pulling out onto the still-quiet road just before seven on a beautiful late summer morning he knew there would be too much accompaniment for him to safely travel the main route. He searched for the promised egress off to the left in the tumultuous granite-carved and bush-hidden terrain and found what he believed was it after five minutes of anxious scanning.

He had to pull to the right onto a slight turnout to let all traffic dissipate. For some reason he felt it safer to do the manoeuvre without witnesses and waited two full minutes until he was alone by both directions.

At first the track was easily traceable and even though the climbs were extreme in comparison to what he and the '42 had hitherto experienced they scaled the heights methodically and nonetheless. Traction was an occasional issue as the loose gravel

and exposed boulders caused him to steer precariously to the
sides and sometimes brake hard to back up and try again. There
was a complete absence of human signs — no tire treads or
discarded trash — which told him the road was likely a project
whose purpose was long expired.

The lonely stone road held confines and solitudes that were
of a deeper profundity than had the amber spread of prairie.
After a couple of hours of wheel and clutchwork the altitude
brought a chill he hadn't felt since April. Gulping fluid between
bites of candy bar he noted that the trail such as it was wound
down from here and would likely connect him with a far-off
lake that he could just see and that he understood also involved
a barge trip to get across.

Upon resuming he struggled to keep the truck stable on
a canted downward fishtail course that challenged his ability
to stay upright and avoid road obstacles at the same time. As
difficult as the going got he was proud of himself in his seeming
bottomless ability to adapt. He was even getting used to the
violence of the tossing he and the '42 were enduring. Another
couple of hours until the end of this touchy leg. The afternoon
shadows were still short as he tooled in second gear around a
slow turn and accelerated to nearly as fast as he had gone on
this rough route to climb a grade. The jouncing in the cab was
as pronounced as ever when he too late glanced something in
the road.

Without even a slight chance of averting it he and the
truck bottomed on a particular high point of jagged boulder
and a sound came up that was out of place. The note of the
engine — after a ping-clunk metallic chime — changed in
the instant after.

He braked instantly and cut the ignition. On exiting the
cab he saw the blackness of a 40-weight fluid-pool widening

under the front end. Though he could see little by stooping and peering, his diagnosis of the problem was certainly that at a minimum the oil pan had been ruptured. Likely at least holed. He feared maybe even slit wide open or at least rent long and jagged and crumpled so as to make roadside repair impossible. As he gazed underneath the dripping slowed.

Not a person disposed toward profanity, Robin struggled now to contain at least a despairing cuff of the forehead or a fruitless throwdown of his hat. Even before grabbing the tool box or fixing the jack or plotting any kind of plan he sat upon the running board and let grief convene a five-minute summit in his heart. Pure regret of an unknown and surprising intensity de-motorized him in a way he'd never experienced and had him head in hands near sobbing in the afternoon sun alone on a roadway so far gone and unused it felt like he was the last boy on earth.

And it was just this contemplation that jolted him out of the great trench of rue he'd navigated into. He shook his head and stood up.

He'd always been alone.

He thus sensed the only answer to despondency was determined physical action. He knew not to think about the tasks ahead and the difficulties and the high likelihood of his not succeeding. A wrench in his hand helped. He drummed it hard against his thigh to further self-emphasize his resolve.

He strode around the '42 and took account of the terrain it sat on. It was blocking the trail. Off to the wider side the scant surface was just enough to let another rig get by. He surveyed the spot and got the collapsible shovel he'd packed and cleared as level a workspace as he could manage. After near an hour he felt it might be okay to start up the cooling engine to move it into position with the least amount of manoeuvring and the least amount of running time manageable to avoid damage to an oil-less engine. This he did with gritted teeth.

Before raising the front end to see the truth of his predicament he forced himself to munch down a bag of potato chips and chug a can of lemonade. With near-trembling hands he assembled the jack and began the process. Knowing that the job was not going to be a five-minute under-and-out fix-up he made it good to crawl in the grime by laying down a tarp he'd folded up and stored between the cab and the box some time ago even before this grand trip had begun. A series of large rocks placed at thicker parts of the frame ensured he would not be crushed by jack failure. With further tremblings of hand and shoulder he propelled himself beneath the dirt-smacked underside of the still-cooling engine.

In the dimness — realizing that in the lateness of the day it would be a task getting enough light on this area to operate successfully — he saw right away that the oil pan was indeed cut open. The high barb of granite he'd seen only at the last instant had scored an almost neat incision down the middle of the wide steel tray. The last of the thick oil that had served so well on long climbs dripped lugubriously out the slit.

Though the damage was grave and a remedy did not come immediately to his mind, he took solace from the solid fact he had accurately diagnosed the problem nearly the instant it had occurred. Seeing it now confirmed was a strange consolation to what — if he were not to conquer this terrible turn of misfortune — was otherwise prominent on the list of worst things that could happen. He allowed himself a long sigh and a protracted examination of the whole of the rent by running fingers along it and feeling the still-heated remnant oil lubricate their caress.

Back up and standing he selected the proper ratchet bit and wrench. He found some rags and his only flashlight and fetched the bucket. A quick wrench of the drain plug produced a drip of remaining oil only sufficient to just cover its bottom. It took less than three minutes to dislodge the bolts holding the pan to the bottom of the crankcase and he saw that about a third of a quart was still in the bottom pockets of the part. As he pulled the stuck pan away from its gasket — a part he was trying to preserve as he knew there would be no easy replacement — a slop of oil splatted against his forearm. The heat of it scalded deep. He cried out knowing no one would hear and wondered even through the pain if he would have done so with an audience. He crawled out and gently wiped the wound with a rag and wrapped it with a slightly cleaner rag. The situation called for working through pain and he duly ventured back under the truck without further first aid.

A look by the glint of his flashlight up into the gloom of the engine gave solid relief in that it did not appear that the block was cracked and the piston rods and crankshaft seemed in order and unscarred. He carefully extricated himself and the pan from under the rig so as to pour the inky remnant into the bucket. Once done he made a point of storing the bolts to a special niche in the tool kit. He felt that a near-plodding systematic pace to the repair would be better than panic. He rummaged through the tool kit and the glove compartment and behind and under the seat for anything useful.

The immediate need was a ball-peen hammer and flat surface to straighten out the bent metal and rejoin the lips of the separation. This he set to right away. The search for a perfect flat rock took time. He scanned the road banks for many yards in either direction and tried out several candidates before selecting the best of the collection. Then the set-up of a rock-and-tree-stump workspace. Finally he hammered. The satisfaction of forcing metal to his will reassured at least a temporary sense of proficiency. In a few minutes he had both sides joined in a presentable seam and ideas began to percolate as to how to seal it at least enough to get him off this lonely trail and into a machine shop for proper repair.

A pause to look for materials turned into a snack and water break. The sun warming him was at a low angle and would soon slip behind a near peak. Though it was only mid-afternoon he could almost already feel the altitude chill that dusk and darkness would bring. He tossed a last palmful of salted peanuts into his mouth.

Whether it was a myth or whether it was wisdom he had heard once in a general store oldster's conversation or a spot on television or perhaps a dream that a bar of soap was a handy resource in such a situation. Though he could not remember if this applied only to low-pressure-and-heat fuel tanks or a more general use, he nevertheless tried taking the one piece of Lifebuoy he had and rubbing it across the cut where there were edges to catch. Sure enough the waxy substance filled and conformed to the gaps and cracks. Next came duct tape, of which he had an ample supply. He took pains to scrub both sides of the wound to try to create a slick-free surface. Liberal applications of the all-purpose adhesive to either surface of the pan made the odd assembly appear at least continent.

He slid under and reattached the oil pan with the carefully saved bolts sealing up against the carefully preserved cork gasket. He placed the bucket under the repair to catch failure if it should occur. He fetched the remaining oil supply to mix the small amount of heavier stuff with the used but still good lighter stuff. Once filled he replaced the cap and closed the engine hood as if despite the truck still being up on a jack he was truly getting ready to speed off into the thickening dusk.

He paused for a moment on the seat with key in the ignition and hand on key trying not to think of the weightedness of this moment. Glancing about at the scrub and stone sides of his stopping place he was moved by a desperate resolve to leave. The engine caught immediately and achieved a steady idle. The sound was good. He stepped down from the cab and determined as best he could in the dullness below that nothing was leaking. He let it warm. To be fully sure he knew he would have to up the revs to see if the normal operating pressure might defeat his work. He climbed back in and gave the gas pedal three sessions of increase and then let it idle again and stepped down to have a look.

In the gathering gloom it was nevertheless clear that a steady black stream columned from the bottom of the pan neatly into the perfectly positioned bucket. He cut the motor. As the leak was slow he had to loosen the drain plug at the lowest region of the pan and waited until all the oil in the crankcase was safely in the bucket. When he had the pan once again in his hands he saw that the inner layer of duct tape had detached and been floating about in the hot reservoir. He knew he was fortunate it had not plugged the sump or otherwise fouled itself into the moving parts just above the oil level. The soap seal had completely melted.

Seeing how his innovation had been put asunder he knew that a normal reaction to such a development would be to at least despair a little. Knowing himself, however, he resolved to become even calmer than he'd been forcing himself all that afternoon to be. As dark descended he began to make ready to spend another night in the cab.

The night was moonless and cold as he had thought it would be. He piled clothes and his jacket overtop the sleeping bag to make it warm enough to get to sleep. As he drifted off a coyote yip and far-off howl snapped him alert. He knew he had to try to sleep, and so tried to concentrate on silence. His ears rang with a mystery chime he had never noticed before.

Sunlight came as a surprise. Jolted by dream, he knew it was too early to rise and he accepted with gratitude that through the biological wonders of human sleep he was perfectly toasty under the improvised covers despite the sheen of ice apparent on the windshield.

An hour later he found that if he stood in the sunshine the warmth was fine even with no shirt on and he could stand a wet cloth running through armpits and around grimy neck. The towel he'd laid out on the shaded hood the night before was stiff with frost but he used it anyway. Breakfast would be a piece of stale sandwich left over from dinner and likely a few days old when he'd bought it. He tried not to think of the diner ham and eggs he once had before him on a clean table with knife and fork at the ready. Though his last stop in civilization had only been twenty-four hours ago that life seemed far away.

His burnt arm had been hurting dully through the night and he decided to unwrap it and see if exposure to the air might help the healing. The angry red slightly shocked him. Skin came away with the wrapping. He resolved to find a proper bandage and some disinfectant salve once back in civilization.

As he munched and drank cola he knew that his next move would have to be something he was so loath to consider that he scarcely let himself be rational about it. He began to gather things he would enclose in a backpack preparatory to a hike. By reckoning from the map and the proximity of the lake ahead he figured that the shortest route to help would be ahead and not behind. He wrapped the oil pan in a large rag and positioned it in his pack amid the water bottles and remaining candy bars. He closed the windows and locked the truck doors. Turning away he wish-willed that the next time he saw it there would be no change in its condition. With luck he figured to walk out of this exile to a highway and hitchhike to the nearest service station and get the weld he needed to be back here even perhaps later that day. Perhaps.

Before he strode three steps a motor sound echoed off the surrounding granite. At first unbelieving Robin at least stopped walking to cock an ear to fully analyze the sound. The thrumming surged, faded, then came in strong as a somewhat beat-up Econoline van poked out from the far turn and rolled dustily down toward him. As it slowed he forgot to be elated at his possible reprieve from an uncertain day of walking and warily studied the occupants. The van was driven by a heavy-set middle-aged man accompanied by an attentive mixed-breed dog in the passenger seat.

He locked eyes with the man as the vehicle gently stopped and in that easy handling and the look of a big soft hand on the steering wheel and especially in the even manner of the man's returned gaze Robin received reassurance.

Well, Trouble. The man smiled at his travel companion and turned back to Robin through an open window. Looks like we've found trouble.

The words knocked the logic blocks from beneath Robin's understanding of the world and the situation before him. It took a few embarrassing seconds until his comprehension re-aligned. Is that the name of your dog? Trouble?

Once you get to know him you'll think it's the most perfect title for a mutt ever. The man turned his engine off. And your form of trouble is pretty plain to see. He peered at the jacked-up '42. Transmission?

Oil pan.

Oh that's okay then. We might fix that.

How far is it down there? Robin pointed in his intended direction.

Walking? Oh a good four hours or so to the other road. The one that this leads to. But it isn't much more than this one. Then in either direction if you don't get a ride — which likely you'll not because it's near as lonely on that road as it is on this one — another oh about four hours just to get where the ferry gets you across Arrow Lake. Is that where you were going?

I guess. I didn't really know for sure.

Well it's the only good route to take if you're looking for a repair because I can't think of any other type service you'd get much before Lumby. That's if you want to go west. Going north you'd likely find something at Nakusp.

Gee. I don't want to go to either of those places. I just want to get my truck fixed.

Well let's see about that. The man opened his door. The dog immediately jumped over him, licked Robin in several places, barked happily, and ran in all directions. The man stepped out of the van offering his hand. Name's John.

Robin.

Well, Robin, what brings a young boy like you out here to Valhalla?

Valla-what?

That's the name of this reserve we're sitting in right now. The southern rim of it anyway.

I didn't know that.

The name means some kind of heaven to the Norse people.

It's some kind of hell to me. Can't wait to get out.

Well there's better ways. This one here is a forest road. Others are service roads. Only open for a few months of the year. There are easier ways to go.

I like going where nobody else goes.

Well I can get behind that. Kind of the same myself. He peered at Robin grinningly. And I suppose you'd rather not be located by any kind of authority.

Nope.

So you cross the country underground so to speak. Only on these near-deserted goat trails.

Yup. And I'm only travelling at night. At least from now on.

Have you had adventures?

Sure. Close ones.

John gestured to the '42. Is this one of the close ones?

You could say that.

John kicked at the nasty spur in the middle of the road and looked at the oily patch beyond it. I guess this is where you scraped, eh?

Yup.

What was the damage?

Robin unshouldered his pack and dug out the part.

Aha ... John ran a finger along the creased gap. And of course it's an antique or nearly that. Old metal. High carbon, low alloy. Could be welded but ultimately you'd want to get a new used part. Off a wreck somewhere. If you could find one.

Likely the part'll be the same off other years. But right now I have to get this crack plugged.

Yes you do. John peered at the wound on Robin's arm. I don't like the look of that either. How long has it been angry?

Since yesterday when I did it. Hot oil.

Uh-huh. John went to a box at the side door of his van and rummaged. Let me put some salve on it. Might stop infection at least.

Whether intended to or not the application immediately calmed the tender area. John wrapped the arm in gauze.

Feels a lot better. Thanks.

No problem but let's keep an eye on it … And now let's have a look at this bigger problem here. John stepped to the '42 and bent to look under. Have you got more oil?

Yes.

So have I. So that's not an issue. Tools?

Robin showed John the box and his other implements.

Whoa … you're a travelling repair shop. Even better than me. John strode to the van and opened the rear doors. Here's what I got. Maybe we can cobble something together.

I tried duct tape.

Oh. Yeah that wouldn't hold. Too much glue-breaking. Oil does that every time. And heat and pressure.

I found out.

No. If anything's going to work on this it'll have to be some kind of metal patch. Maybe bolted on. Maybe soldered.

I figured.

I got an electric soldering iron but … John comically glanced around the woods. No power.

Yeah I know.

But hold on a sec. John shuffled back to Robin's tool box. You got wood chisels?

Some.

Is there one you can spare? That you don't want anymore?

I don't know.

Well we can get a fire going and ruin one of these doing a solder job after a fashion. I did it once. Kind of worked.

Robin took hold of one of Jimmy Scott's bevelled sharp tools and held it up. Whatever it takes.

We'd have to find some kind of metal for a patch. It'll ideally be a similar grade to whatever it is that your oil pan is made of. Something around the same age at least.

Really?

Yeah. That's my experience. John stepped back and surveyed the '42. Is there any part of this fine old truck you could see cutting off so's you wouldn't miss it?

No. Not at all.

Well. Okay then. I guess we have to get creative. One thing though. John went back to his own collection box. Not absolutely sure I've got the solder. He rummaged for more moments than made Robin comfortable. Aha! He held up a coiled shiny knot. Here it is. Might just be enough.

Gee. It sure would be good if this works.

Well we'll see.

It's awful nice of you to stop like this and lend a hand.

What? John feigned incredulity. You think I'd just roll by a fellow sojourner in trouble out here in the middle of nowhere? His eyes darkened. Speaking of which. Have you seen my dog?

Robin shrugged. Not since you got out of your van.

John lightened. Oh he'll be around. Dinnertime's not far away.

What kind of dog is he anyway?

Oh Trouble? He's every kind of mutt you ever heard of. Though I think he's mostly terrier. What kind of terrier I could not tell you.

He sure is friendly. Reminds me of some farm dogs I've known.

He is that. And a fine travel companion too. Doesn't stink too much. We stop by streams every chance. He loves to go for a dip.

Ha ha. Doesn't anybody else travel with you?

No family with me. Some out on the prairie we're heading to right now. It's my standard summer vacation. Like to take a different mystery route every time. Get bored on the Number One. That's why you see me before you.

I hope I'm not holding you up.

Stops are part of the fun. There's no hold-ups. Just interesting layovers.

I've been laid over here near a full day.

Well, my new friend, I hate to tell you but it's likely you'll be doing another full day before you can bid this place goodbye. We've got a lot of rigmarole to get through first.

I appreciate it.

Have you had lunch?

Nope.

Got any food at all?

Chocolate bars and chips.

You're kidding, right?

Nope. I had to leave my last place in a bit of a hurry. Couldn't quite get prepared.

Well I got beans and bread. For starters.

That sounds fantastic.

Trouble! John called upward as he pulled a box from the interior of the van. Trouble!

A yelp sounded nearby and the mutt emerged from shrub trotting enthusiastically toward them. Well now that the third member of our dinner party is here I'll get this camp stove going and warm up the can.

I sure appreciate this.

John turned to Robin with a can and opener in hand. Helping is the last pure thing humans can do in the final account. The only thing that lasts. The best and most essential act that puts us ahead. He handed the can and opener to him. Now see to this and I'll get the cooker started.

They munched baked beans and bread and apples that John had in a cooler. Another cooler had ice and cod fillets within. John placed it where the sun would not get to it.

That's for dinner.

You sure have good provisions.

Have to. I like to travel off-road but I have to manage diabetes too.

Oh?

John slapped his potbelly. Yup. Take my advice youngster, don't get old and fat. Old is fine and inevitable. Just not fat at the same time.

Robin smiled. I wouldn't say you're fat. Husky maybe.

You should have seen me five years ago. When I drove off the road in a blood-sugar coma. Nearly died. They told me to lose forty pounds and go on insulin.

Wow.

Darn right. It sobered me up pretty quick I'll tell you. So I lost the weight. And then I didn't have to use the needle. Keep it under control with diet and exercise. John laughed. Or maybe just diet. He threw a dog treat to Trouble. The dog jumped to expertly catch it mid-air. He gets enough exercise for both of us.

Ha.

But speaking of old. That tool box of mine was given to me by my father.

Yeah?

So it's a good thirty or so years old. Your truck is —

— twenty-five —

— years old. So maybe we can take a piece off the lid there for our patch job.

No. Your dad gave it to you.

He'd want it to go to the best use.

We might wreck it.

There's a way we can do it. I'm thinking that the underside is good for our purpose. Paint's long been worn away.

I guess that's important.

Yep. Well. John stood up off the tailgate where they'd been sitting. Guess there's no time like the present.

I'll start gathering wood.

You do that. And load it over there in that clear bit away from the trees. We'll have to be damn careful. As little smoke as possible. We don't want the whole ranger service coming down here and accusing us of starting a forest fire.

When Robin had gathered and roughly chopped as much wood as he felt might be necessary to start and maintain a hot fire he saw that John had worked with tin snips to carefully extricate a perfect strip of metal from the lid of his own tool kit. He wondered if he would ever become blasé about the sacrifices others made for him and resolved in the moment to try never to take anything like this for granted. He found himself oddly fighting back tears as they set about building a fire and placed John's lawn chairs around it to tend and enjoy the heat and cheer it provided.

They found that the job entailed heating not only the sacrificial chisel to act as an impromptu soldering iron but that the two metals would not bind unless both were heated almost glowing. This entailed one or other of them to hold the part over the coals with an improvised pair of tongs made by duct-taping a wrench and a screwdriver together. When sufficiently heated they fused the patch metal onto the crack by melting and pressing the solder metal as firmly as possible with the aid of a hammer and work gloves. It was a co-operative effort that demanded coordination that they both took to without much adjustment.

The process was slow. They were well toward evening before the job approached completion so dinner took priority. John cooked fish and roasted fresh corn over the fire and they

brewed tea and ate cookies for dessert. Then they worked in the
fire-lit darkness to finish the oil pan. Robin was encouraged by
the results and felt none of the trepidation he'd held when trying out his earlier repair attempt.

It's too dark to do any more. Let's sit down awhile and yack
a bit before bed.

Okay.

You have a bed don't you?

I sleep in the cab when it's cold.

Kind of cramped, isn't it? John ruffled Trouble's ears and
rubbed at his furry neck with both hands. You can bed down with
us in the van if you want. At least you'll be able to lie out straight.

Okay. But the cab's not too cramped. Not yet at my height
so far anyway. The box is best but it can get cramped too.

Oh?

I had a girl crawl in with me a few nights ago. Robin found
that he desperately desired to talk about what was on his mind.
It got real cramped then.

Oho! Do tell.

She was at one of those hitcher camps.

Aw, a free-love hippie girl. The best kind.

Well I don't know about that.

What don't you know? Didn't you …

The question hung in the air unfinished and unanswered.

We just talked.

But you liked her and she liked you and she came un-
requested into your bed?

Naked.

Naked!

That was about it. She was so nice …

And nothing happened?

We talked all night. Well. Most of the night.

You talked.

Yeah. We talked.

Wait a minute wait a minute wait a minute … John guffawed and shifted position in his chair. You mean to say a girl crept naked as a Botticelli into your parlour and you lay calm and perfectly chaste beside her all night?

Well … I don't know about a bottle-something. And it was my sleeping bag she crawled into but … Yeah.

Botticelli painted a lot of pretty girls. And I meant parlour figuratively, boy.

Okay.

And you didn't do anything with her?

She offered and everything. But she was okay with just talking.

John shook his head laughing. Born yesterday were you, son?

I think she just wanted a friend to be close to her.

Sure about that?

I'm not sure about anything. Maybe it was more what I wanted. I just liked getting to know her really well.

Oh I'm sure she wanted that too. Just not in a strictly verbal way.

Well yeah. Maybe.

She was looking for more and you didn't give it to her? John paused, gazing into the fire. She's good looking, right?

Sure is.

Well in a situation like that just a lot of talk is not normally what happens.

I know. But something told me it should be different. With her.

Ha ha ha … You're an okay kid, Robin. Whatever anybody will ever say. But I'll tell you one thing. Manna from heaven doesn't flow like that every day, my boy.

It wasn't like that. Deep down I don't think she wanted me to do anything with her other than be a good friend.

Women send signals, boy.

Her signal was "just be nice."

This one was holding up a neon sign by the sound of it.

She was pretty direct all right.

So what were you waiting for? An engraved invitation?

I just didn't feel like we were ready.

Well ... John straightened his legs in a stretch and gazed up into the star-littered heavens. There is something to be said for relationship. Consideration. Sharing.

I think I knew that.

Well hear this and make of it what you will. In my experience, if you make love to a woman she tends to fall in love with you. Whatever your true feelings for her. She likes you enough to listen to your talk and grant access to her body. Average woman in that position is left with love in her heart. It's kind of a human element. Women get fond of people and things close to them. Remember this. If you just have sex with them and then right away go away they get sad. And there's nothing like the sadness of a woman to rend the heart of a good man. If you are good. So hurting women ... there's no excuse for such a thing. To be avoided at all costs. There's already enough hurt in the world.

I think I knew that too.

You're quite a young fella. To be grasping it all.

We're going to meet up. Aldis and me. A couple of months from now.

Oh? Did she give you an address and a specific time?

October in Victoria. And a phone number.

Well that's something. John smiled over at Robin. As a veteran of two marriages I'm rooting for you, boy. But a couple of words of advice. I know you're considerate. You've got manners and a good regard for others. And your treat-ment of females so far sounds exemplary and that's bound to make your life a whole lot more tranquil than most. But remember this. There's a time to discard ceremony and grab what you need. Try to distinguish between need and want. That's important too. Watch out for the times want gets you in the gut. But either way. Understand your needs. There will be a time not to be polite.

A moment passed while Robin mentally rummaged for a reply. Uh … okay. If you say so.

I say so my boy from hard and bitter experience. Since we have all the time in the world and neither of us are going any-where for the next day or so anyway, I'll tell you about it.

There was a silence and the crackle of the fire.

I appreciate any advice you have. Sounds like you come by it from hard experience.

You might say that.

What do you do for a living?

I'm a kind of social worker. I help mistaken fellows get through prison and out the other side.

Oh. Mistaken?

There are so many ways you can go wrong, Robin.

I'm getting that idea, yeah.

Oh I'd venture you're just getting started at life lessons. But keep a positive outlook and you'll do fine.

What got you going working with criminals?

The notion that there but for the grace of the collective goodness of mankind went I. There were times I could have ended up in jail. Especially during the war.

You were in the war?

Navy. Did most of my hitch on the Murmansk run. Do you know what that was?

I think we read a bit about it in history class last term. World War Two, right?

Double-U double-U two, that's right.

Where's Murmansk?

Up past Norway heck and gone into the near perma-frozen Barents Sea is where it is. For us it was the only port we could off-load all the supplies Russia needed to lick the Germans. We escorted the freight-haulers up there for as many trips as we had personnel and ships and time to do it.

And you could have gone to jail for that?

Naw, kid. We were crazy sailors risking our lives. Ashore we were menaces to society.

Drinking and stuff?

Oh if it had only been drinking and stuff. You put men in that position ... Naval action is a special thing in the first place. The Murmansk run was special beyond that. In a war like that one on a smaller ship you face certain death a large percentage of the time. Whole ships' companies were lost. The water between England and Russia — winter or summer — is cold enough to kill you in minutes if the guns or torpedoes or drowning or whatever else doesn't get you. And it's always rough up there, weather-wise. A tough sail any way you slice it. So we were near berserk with tension by the time we got off a monthlong circuit. I saw guys drive cars into buildings and break up shops and pick fights with elderly men. People I would otherwise respect going absolutely haywire. Good thing there were shore police. I got caught one time stealing a sausage out of a broken window and sat in the brig for a week. Sobered me up, I'll tell you. Got me to thinking about life and what I thought it meant. Etcetera. I won't bore you with the details.

It's sure not boring. You're the second guy I've run into who was in the war.

Oh? Heh. I guess some of us are still walking around with our heads still attached but spinning. I'm okay though.

I can tell.

And I like what I'm doing. I tried other stuff. Once owned a string of taxi cabs. That was fun.

Oh yeah?

You get to be prince of the city. To a ridiculous degree, considering what it actually is and isn't. But ... even that can get boring.

I can't stand being bored.

It's the worst thing ... or near the worst that can happen to a fellow. For sure. Second only perhaps to not getting an education.

Oh?

If I hadn't got to go to university after the war — Veteran's Affairs paid for it — I'd be nowhere near the engaging, well-rounded personality I am today. Heh heh.

No kidding?

Well sort of kidding but there's a lot to it. My advice to a young guy like you. Once you're finished this here hegira you seem to be on. Go to school.

I'm going into Grade Ten when I get to the coast.

You do that. And stick with it no matter what.

I thought I would.

It's one of the things that keeps me going in correctional work. I was in a meeting one day with an array of cops from around the country and one of them came up with a statistic on the number of children who feared violence at school. Violence at school. They didn't go to school because they didn't want to get beat up or they did go to school and expected to get beat up. It was then I knew I was in the right business.

Were most of your criminals bullies?

We call them clients. Yeah. They were bullies and they were bullied. The idea is to interrupt the cycle. Their stories are always more complicated than you expect.

Sounds interesting at least.

It surely is. It's us adults finishing an upbringing for other adults that didn't get a proper one in the first place. All kinds of reasons. But when you talk about children who go astray it's not just them that has to answer. It's the parents, society, the government, the whole world. Everybody bears responsibility.

I never thought about it like that.

Well there's personal culpability beyond that. At a certain stage.

How so?

You've got to make sure you take responsibility, Robin. Things happen beyond your control — glad or sad — that's all bad or good. But once the die is cast you take the deal. Hold yourself responsible. You're the one that chose. Stand with it. Be a man.

Robin sat silent.

Yup. John sipped his tea as the fire crackled. He gazed again to the star-speckled sky. And in your life you will do the things that make up a remembered biography. You will save a life in both the corporeal and spiritual realm. Maybe save a little old lady from a burning house. Heroin addict from his last deadly fix. You will try to express yourself to the greater world with little or no understanding of that greater world. You will travel. You might sit in Rothko's Seagram Murals room in the Tate gallery and feel the psychic vibrations the artist meant for you over the span of time and the chasm of mortality. You might drive madly across cities with people's lives in your hands. Women will love and despise you. Your footsteps might echo off the ancient walls of a deserted Italian piazza at four in the morning ...

John's words had become miasmic as Robin began to dream and realized he had been dozing and dream-remembering an earlier speech he had witnessed as part of a life-lesson. He managed a grunted acknowledgement that John had stopped speaking and arose. I gotta go to bed.

Good idea.

. . .

Morning began with Trouble licking his face so wetly Robin thought through dream that he was taking a shower.

Pah! He rolled from the sleeping bag wiping his face. He'd been stretched out in the van after all and the side door was open.

Ha ha … Morning there, sleepyhead. Trouble doesn't like anybody lying in past his wake time. John was puttering about the fire site. The sound of frying came to Robin's ears at the same time the smell of bacon hit him. He pulled up his pants.

John poured pancake batter into a frying pan full of bacon grease. Sure is a fine morning. He looked to the sky with spatula in hand. Feels like a good one to work on motors.

I sure hope it is. Cup in hand Robin sat in a lawn chair and leaned to pour coffee from a pot warmed by the fire. He had again not let himself think about what it meant if the laborious repair they'd performed yesterday would not hold. But whatever. Breakfast sure smells good.

Well here's a plate. John handed him a platter with bacon and a sliced tomato on it. He dished from the pan the large pancake he'd been cooking. There you go.

They ate and sat around the dying fire and with only a distant memory of living anywhere else Robin gazed about the surroundings now as if they were more like home. I've been here two days. I hated the place at the beginning and I still don't particularly like it.

Clashes with your concept of freedom despite the beauty and tranquility. It's how prisons work. Even if they were pleasant, anybody confined anywhere comes to resent where it is they can't leave. Just human nature.

I guess.

Someday you might roll back through here just for nostalgia sake and point out this little camp and tell people you had a fine time here with a guy you met on the road and wonder whatever happened to.

Actually. I'd like to keep in touch. I don't even know where you live.

Right now it's East Vancouver. Sometimes it's Deep Cove. If you want I'll let you know occasionally where it is.

Oh for sure.

Heh heh … Your address book is filling up. But remember. If you lose anyone's lose mine and make sure it's not that cute young girl's that's after you.

I'm trying not to think about her right now.

Wise. It'll be a while before you see her.

Yeah.

There's nothing worse than a guy who's pining over some lost love or other.

I guess.

And we have important work ahead of us.

Robin put aside his empty plate. I'll get right under there and bolt it back up.

It's a one-man job, all right. But you're just trying to get out of doing the dishes.

Oh hey I'll do them. Robin stood.

Oh for crying out loud I was just joking.

Mid-job Robin was pleased that the oft-removed gasket appeared to have maintained cohesion. He had half the bolts finger-tightened when Trouble appeared and began ardently licking his face again.

Ach!

That dog sure likes you.

He's living up to his name.

You wouldn't want to take him along, would you? Not convinced he's all that attached to me.

I got no way to keep care of him. Robin shifted and spat. It's all I can do to take care of myself.

You do fine.

And get serious. He's your dog, John.

Alas. It is true.

Robin tightened the bolts with estimated precision. Given his experience with all manner of farm equipment the importance of getting equal tension on all six bolts without the assistance of a torque wrench was not lost on him. He slid out. Well. I guess we test.

Above him John had pulled the oil cap off and now carefully refilled the crankcase. He twisted it tight. Pull those blocks out. Lower the jack.

Should we? What if it doesn't hold?

Then we're going somewhere we can get a tow to a proper garage where they can get you either another part or repair that one and likely have to make you a new gasket because that one will fall apart if it's removed one more time. John looked up and down the lonely road they stood upon and then fixed a firm look at Robin. Besides, boy. You gotta have faith.

Faith.

Yup.

Robin slipped behind the wheel and felt a tinge of non-familiarity at the realization he had not been driving this vehicle for nearly two days that with the goodly slice of life and effort in the interim felt like much longer. With John gazing at him from the middle of the road he turned the key without contemplation and was at least pleased to hear the engine he had tuned so far ago in Saskatchewan catch immediately. He let it idle and listened closely to the note while scanning John's face for a reaction to what he saw below. After half a minute he got out of the truck and crouched to see.

John spoke before he could focus. She's holding so far.

Yeah looks like. But the real test is revs.

Let 'er warm up a bit. Then we'll know.

They stood for three minutes listening to the rumble and monitoring the gravel below the oil pan. Robin tried not to wince at the fact that any leak would not be caught by a basin below. In his mind he tried to accept the venturesome spirit John was advocating but he could barely stand it. Should we get the bucket?

Same thing as the gasket. If this doesn't work you'll be getting new stuff. Cleaner is better anyway.

Yeah.

Well. Time to rev 'er up.

Figure?

Oil'll be hot enough by now.

Robin stepped with palpable trepidation to the cab door.

Wait a minute. John stepped toward him. Let me do it. You look. It's more your concern than whether or not the thing runs.

Okay.

Robin crouched and tried not to cringe as John gunned the engine long and loud and let it wind down and then gunned it again and again.

John stepped to the roadway and peered under. How'd we do?

Nothing showing.

That's good.

Yup.

We're geniuses.

I still have to drive it all the way out of here. And try not to do the same thing around the next bend.

Just be careful. And slow. There's no hurry.

The '42 sat running as they doused the fire and gathered the lawn chairs. Robin piled his stuff into the cab and slapped closed his tool box.

When both had completely packed up they took a long look again at the bottom of the truck's engine. There was no sign of leakage.

Well I guess you're on your way.

I guess. I can't thank you enough, John.

It's been a lot of fun, Robin. John pointed up the road. Like I said. It's a couple of hours for you until the service road ends and you're on a provincial secondary. It's not far then to the ferry. You just roll on, it's a highways connector so there's no fare to pay. If you get there at night for the last one — around ten o'clock or so — it'll be dark enough for you to pull it off. Wear your hat low.

That was my plan.

John stepped to the van and took a paper bag out of the cooler. Here's a sandwich.

Gee. Thanks.

Look me up when you get to the big city.

I will.

I never asked where you were going.

The island. After that I don't know.

Well you're a good man. Whatever happens I'm sure it'll all work out.

I hope so. But one more thing ...
What's that?
What does hedge-ear-ah mean?
Heh heh. Hegira. Go to school and you'll find out.
They shook hands.

Robin waited until the Econoline had fired up and was edging down the slight incline. Seeing that John was waiting for him to also get moving he put the '42 in gear and gently pulled out of the turnout. Both waved as they disappeared from rear-view mirror range.

The terrain did not change in its threat to disassemble any machine whose operator did not observe the strictest care in avoiding ledges and boulder-strewn ditches and sharpened mid-road outcroppings. Robin drove with solemn precision and a constant eye on temperature and oil pressure. He tenderly navigated around any rock that seemed high and only once had a heart-seize moment when the differential knocked solidly on something he thought he'd cleared. But the power seemed uninterrupted to the wheels and the stick shift still availed him all the gears. He continued without stopping.

It took more time than expected but he was nonetheless elated to see from a sharp turn high on a ridge that the road came out below onto a two-lane country highway. He pulled under a clump of maples just out of sight from the pavement and settled for the wait until dark. The sandwich John had packed for him went down well as he watched late afternoon turn to evening. He used the downtime to first check the oil — no leakage whatsoever from the repair — and pump the remnants of farm gas from out of the bed reserve. He considered grimly that the near-full load in the '42's tank would be good for a night's travel but from now on until he needed to drive no more he would require service station stops.

By the map he saw where the ferry was and estimated how long it might take to get there on the road before him. Then he took a nap in anticipation of a long grind through the night. When it was dark he pulled onto the tarmac and near audibly rejoiced at the feeling of smooth pavement below. In twenty-five minutes he rolled up to a line of cars waiting for the cable ferry. Though there were ample overhead lights down the loading ramp and onto the deck he found it fine to keep his face obscured by shadow.

Once back on the road the cars with him on the crossing turned off within a few miles. He was largely alone driving along the darkened main streets of Kelowna and crossed the long pontoon bridge nearly solo.

Up in the hills along the lakeside he found an all-night gas station. The attendant topped up the '42 sleepily and took the exact change handed him without looking.

As early light rose from behind, Robin approached the by-pass route around Princeton and decided through sleepiness and the rising light that it was time to find a hiding place. On the other side of town there were several light industrial businesses including a vast wrecking yard. He pulled the truck in behind some of the derelict cars stacked two and three high beyond the fence. Parking in a distant wooded spot that looked like it had not been traversed by man or vehicle for years camouflaged boy and truck perfectly.

Sleep came immediately, despite the persistent semi-trailer traffic rumbling by on the highway. He woke to bright sunshine through the back window and the heat of the day making him sweaty. Hunger was a factor. He set out on foot for the restaurant he'd seen in the darkness and found it busy with a lunch crowd of truckers and hard-hatted highway maintenance personnel. After a hearty bowl of soup and a burger with fries chased down with coffee and pie he was feeling hale. Gazing from the counter stool he could swivel full around and watch traffic whizz by on the roadway to rejoice that he was once again among people and civilization.

Though drawn toward a stroll downtown he knew the next order of important vehicular business would have to be to address the possible impending failure of the mountainside oil pan repair. He'd glanced at the underside this morning and had seen nothing immediately concerning — the dipstick indicated the level was up where it should be — but he was troubled by a bead of dark fluid that hung from the region of damage.

He walked the long fence along the wrecking yard that traced around a corner and back to a crude driveway, ending in a padlocked chain-link gate. A dog of indeterminate breed but definite belligerence cantered up and barked peevishly at him through the woven steel.

Nice doggy.

She is anything but a nice doggy.

Robin was near startled by the presence nearby of a shaggy bearlike man swathed in grimy plaid and holed denim. Oh. Robin spoke through metal grate. Well. I wasn't planning on finding out.

What were you planning on?

I'm looking for a part.

Yuz are, are yuz?

Yup.

Well. The man undid the lock with a key from a collection on a lanyard around his neck. Step careful.

Robin noted numerous dog droppings as he walked through the swung-open gate and several more avid canines of varied background bounded close.

The man sized him openly as his dogs did a thorough sniff-around.

They probably smell Trouble on me.

Oh?

I mean a dog named Trouble. Not trouble trouble.

How do we know for sure?

Ha ha, well I guess you'll have to get to know me.

Not likely. What kind of part are we talking?

Nineteen thirties-forties Chev half-ton pickup. I need an oil pan.

GM, you're talking.

Right.

And what year exactly?

Forty-two.

Hmmm. Not likely to have that one. Might have a previous.

They were all similar in the thirty-seven to forty-two models. And they kept the same design from forty-six and after for a while. I've seen pictures.

You don't say.

But I don't hope to find the exact part. Maybe just a repair or something to modify.

Well let's see ... The wrecker strolled into a small outbuilding. Robin followed. Inside it was clear that this was the nerve centre of the massive yard. Cluttered arrangements of auto parts and knick-knacks and paper and mechanic manuals. Though intent on his mission Robin did note an irregular adornment theme for the walls. Where the usual cheesecake posters and calendar photos of scantily clad women brandishing power tools would usually be, there were instead framed reproductions of what he took to be famous men. Mostly tweed-clad gentry with nineteenth-century beards. The wrecker pulled down a battered ledger from an overladen shelf and opened it atop the detritus on the desk. I got a section out back I haven't walked over in so damn long. Might

have those years in it. He flipped pages. Several seconds went
by. You got tools?

Yeah. No. Not on me.

I'll lend you a wrench. The wrecker yanked a drawer and
with one hand extracted a hefty ratchet arm and several socket
sizes. Likely it'll take a five-eights. But take this six-nine too,
just in case. He handed Robin the tools and pointed out the
door of the shed. Take your first right and then go three sections down and then a left. There's your years in there somewhere so take a look. If you need something moved come on
back here and I'll get the forklift. Okay?

Great.

Robin strode solitary into the dead vehicle assemblage and
right away received a sensation of being the privileged entrant
to some kind of multi-era majestic mechanized museum.
Mottled cars and trucks of every rusting character were on
paint-peeled display. A whole history of the world he scarcely
knew was galleried in the vast random alloy amalgam. He
observed the phases of decrepitude and the curious variations
of how surface greenery clambered up and into some vehicles
and others not. There were wafting scents of earth-melded
hydrocarbon. The haphazard feature of glass — some units
maintaining panes and others piteously bereft — told of van-
dalism and/or traffic mishap. Everywhere the suggestion of
painful mortality was leavened by yawning invitations to be
fascinated.

Around the corners and along the course he'd been directed
he eventually perceived to have arrived at the model type and
period of his seeking. Numbers of derelict early-century pick-
ups sat or leaned wheel-less or doorless or glassless or shotgun
shot through. Most had been engine-shorn and this discour-
aged him deeply until he happened upon a heap of sole engines

reposing in a near-pyramid of confused gear. With rising interest he poked around and pried and pushed over heavy rolling
blocks so back-wobbly he had to leap out of their bucking way.
At last a likely candidate revealed itself in a way he could ef-
fectively wrench the ossified bolts and tenderly pull the piece
away from the main body in an effort to preserve the ever-rare
and precious cork gasket. A remaining sheen of lubricant still
preserved the inside from rust.

Back at the shed the wrecker had cooked himself a great mug
of coffee and sat with feet up on the littered desk sipping cau-
tiously through steam. Robin strode in and placed the oil pan
where the man could examine it without shifting position. He
laid the tools down on the seat of the only free chair in the room.

Found something, eh?

I'm pretty sure it's a fit. Might not be the exact year. But.

Okay. You take it away and try it. Doesn't fit you bring it back.

Okay.

How's five dollars?

How about three?

You got exact change?

Yeah.

Three fifty.

Robin pulled bills and counted out coins.

Thanks. The man sat up in his chair and carefully placed
the brimming mug to one side. You a collector? He slid the
money into a desk drawer.

Nope. Only own one thing. A forty-two Chev pickup.

Well. This might cure its ills for now.

I'm hoping.

You from around here?

No.

Where from?

Saskatchewan.

Where you going?

Long Beach. I think.

Oh. Hippie, are you?

Nope.

Aw, come on. Why not? Hippies got the right idea.

I don't know. Hadn't thought about it.

Well. If you're not a hippie and you're travelling overland how are you going?

Driving the forty-two.

The truck, you mean? The one you need this part for?

Yes.

Ha ha ha … You mean you're driving this collector's piece across the country like it's a normal thing to do? Like it's a mode of personal transportation?

That's right.

Is it all fancy restored like?

Nope. Just more or less like it was when it was a farm truck.

No kidding. The wrecker sat back in his chair smiling widely and somehow managed a big slurp of coffee but did not seem to burn his mouth nor spill a drop from the oversize mug. That's pretty damn cool.

Well thanks. I figure so.

Respect. The man leaned across the desk and extended a greasy hand. Name's Clint.

Robin.

They shook.

I appreciate your whole effort. Flight. Something I think everybody's thought of once or twice in a lifetime but never did.

A man told me something like that not long ago.

Well he was right. I appreciate knowing what you're doing just for the understanding that someone out there has a practical respect for what these rolling artifacts represent. And that you're not one who accumulates these creations as baubles to be kept shiny and protected in climate-controlled mausoleums.

Heck no.

But there's an historic-philosophical element too. They are the form-and-function artistic manifestation of a singular industrial heritage. Ever consider that?

Uh. I just like to drive the thing.

Exactly. That breed of power plant is an efficient and finely compromised piece of pragmatic engineering designed to afford you maximum freedom of movement and employability. It fills a need integral to human progress particular to this continent. It'll move a sizable general cargo. It'll run on the most basic gasoline. It has a heater to keep you warm and ventilation enough to let wind swirl from the windows to keep you cool. It has range and a radio.

Mine doesn't. It never worked.

Well. Another need of repair. You want we find you one around here?

I just need to get going.

Fair enough. Got everything you need?

Think so.

Well. Okay. Maybe see you again sometime.

Maybe.

Back at his concealed parking place Robin set to immediate work. Versed in the procedure as he was it wasn't long before he had the new part securely bolted. His confidence pouring oil into the crankcase was affirmed by the sight of no drip at the bottom even after five minutes of idling. He tossed the old part into the bed to serve as a memento. To have accomplished an end to the trouble of the mountains was more of a relief down in the pits of him than he had ever expected.

The feeling of freedom was so good he decided to take a walk around the town and browse through the shops and act like a normal person for a change. He found a pinball arcade where the whiling away of a couple of fun hours only cost him a dollar and a half. On the way back he stopped again at the diner and had the dinner special hot turkey sandwich with an ice-cream-shaped scoop of mashed potatoes and cherry cobbler for dessert.

Striding back to the truck he felt perfectly fine. A far-off sighting of the '42's passenger door ajar took the warmth away in an instant. He jogged the rest of the way.

Robin well understood that the locks on these old duffers were seldom used and not reliable anyway. But having no other method to secure valuables, he'd had no choice but to put his dubious trust in them. When he pulled the door full open he saw what he expected to see. Belongings rifled through and the tool box gone. By the look of things tools were the only essentials missing. He scowled and struck a tree with a closed fist. Then he examined the door to see how entry had been gained but could find no sign of harm. The thief or thieves knew that the lock could be defeated simply — in this case likely just jamming down the window a fraction and pulling up the door handle with a modified coat hanger. He was at least thankful that no damage had been done. Just to be sure he slid behind the wheel and started the motor. All normal. He breathed.

Awaiting outer darkness and as the moon rose in a near autumn sky he calculated the vulnerabilities he now faced without the implements to do repairs on the road. For want of a wrench he could not even change oil. Thankfully the jack and lug-nut puller were still in their places behind the seat. The distance left to go before he would have any kind of workspace was not great but yet undefined. From now on luck would have to play an even larger part. In a darkened mood he fired up and pulled out of the blind.

• • •

Having studied the map, Robin knew he was close to having to find an alternate route around the multiple municipalities of greater Vancouver. He had heard of the rough route being developed via Lillooet over to the coast by way of a gravel road through mountains and past a ski hill toward the sea. He calculated that the town of Squamish would have the necessary services he needed to put in place the only plan he'd had in mind as a method of crossing the Georgia Strait.

He drove with determination north through more mountainous territory and by midnight gassed up in the all-night gasbar town of Spences Bridge. Two hours later he rolled through the slumbering streets of Lillooet and immediately found the only route west by the sobering presence of warning signs stating that the route was rough and there were no services for eighty miles. He calculated that the '42 could go at least a hundred and twenty on what was in the tank so did not hesitate on his way through town to barrel straight on and commit to the challenge of a partially formed road.

Being the veteran of farm access and range track and even mountain-goat trails he found the going not as grinding as the signs would have him believe. He wheeled carefully over open wood bridges without railings. There were freshly graded side-lanes close to open ditches and bubbling creeks. All night he saw few other vehicles. After about fifty miles the road became a paved two-lane throughway passing small settlements. He rolled into the wakening town of Squamish at dawn. Parking on a residential street and gazing up at the imposing granite wall the town featured on one side, he turned to the inlet just visible above rooftops to the west and revelled in a salt breeze on his face he had not felt in years.

Strolling the sidewalk he examined particular residences for signs of desolation. After a half hour he strode into the business centre and found a phone booth. He saw by a clock tower on top of a building that it was shortly after eight. The phonebook displayed several ads for local moving companies. He dialled the first one listed.

After letting fifteen rings go by without an answer he dialled the second number.

In seconds a voice addressed him.

Hi I'm looking for a day's rental on a five-ton truck for a Vancouver Island delivery.

You are, are you ... Well. It isn't quite the end of the month so we might be able to help you. When do you need it?

Today. As soon as possible.

Whoa. Not sure I could raise a crew on short notice.

I don't need a crew. Just a guy to drive the truck.

No crew? What are we loading?

One item. A big one. Easy to handle though.

Okay ... Well I guess I could do the job then. It'll be a pretty penny though. I have to get an Island permit. Then there's the ferry there and back. Whereabouts on the Island?

Qualicum Beach.

Hmmm. Let me see. That's gonna run you a good sixty dollars or so.

I'll have it in cash.

Okay then. What's the address?

Three-seven-nine-six-five Fourth Avenue.

What's your name?

Robin Wallenco.

Okay I'll get you to spell that when I see you.

I'll be out front.

Right. Okay. I have to gas up the truck and do some other stuff. How about ten-thirty? We can get the twelve-thirty ferry if it's a quick load.

I'll be there.

Robin splurged on a long breakfast at a waterside café and ate with an eased mind in the knowledge there was not much of value left in the '42 should someone else take a notion to break into it. Fish boats sallied past his viewpoint and the mill across the inlet spewed smoke. A water taxi ferried workers back and forth to the worksite. His memory of growing up a coastal kid was returning as the imprint of the prairies faded from his mind.

The stroll back to the '42 was pleasant in the sunshine. He found the truck unmolested. Before approaching he surveyed the street both ways and the near side street for pedestrians and any other traffic. He waited until all ways were clear before hopping in and starting up and steering around a corner to the end of the street. Then a turn left and a sweep up onto the grassy boulevard in front of his chosen quiet house. It was as vacant as he'd perceived it a few hours earlier. He gathered his stuff from the cab and loaded it all into a large garbage bag and tossed it into the box. At slightly after ten-thirty a five-ton truck with "Bad Dog Moving & Storage" painted in large letters on each side pulled up. A wiry middle-aged man got out of the cab.

Are you Robin Wallenco?

I am. He nodded to the '42. Here's the freight.

This thing? The man peered at the truck and back at Robin. People usually use a trailer for this kind of thing.

My dad sent me over here to pick this one up. It just got delivered from Saskatchewan by train.

Oh yeah?

It'll be a restoration job but he doesn't want anything more to happen to it if you know what I mean.

So he sent you.

Yup.

Well … I guess we can do it but I gotta know this is your property. The man peered at the quiet house. These people home?

I don't think so. They're the ones who brokered the deal. My dad flew out to the prairies and bought it and got it registered. Want to see the papers?

I guess I oughta.

Robin pulled the registration from the glove compartment. My dad's name is the same as mine.

I think the way it goes is your name is the same as your dad's.

Oh. Yeah I guess.

The man glanced at the papers. Is it operational?

Sure is.

But your dad didn't want to drive it all the way out here from the prairies, eh?

Nope. That's a long way. Not even sure this baby would even make it.

Yeah. He handed the registration back. Well I guess we got to figure how it gets into that there cargo box. I'm thinking I'll back it.

You'll have to squeeze out the side window and crawl over the hood to get out. But it should work.

Oh yeah it'll work. We done this kinda stuff before. Is that bed tank empty?

Yes it is.

Okay it better be. Illegal to transport dangerous substances in this way. Is the truck's gas tank empty too?

Almost.

Just enough to drive it into the truck. No more. Or as close to that as possible. I'll assume that's what.

Do you want me to drive it on?

You're too young to drive, aren't ya?

I drove it on the farm we found it on.

Yeah but. Around here you'd be in trouble if the Mounties came around. Better we do this legal as possible.

The loading went quicker than expected. The moving man opened the wide cargo doors and positioned a ramp so that the '42 could be backed into the box without repositioning. Robin saw immediately that the mover was an expert with machines. The task was completed in less than ten minutes and to Robin's relief attracted no attention on the street. When the cargo doors closed it was as if there never had been an antique truck parked there.

Before the Sun Was Gone

THOUGH IT HAD BARELY REACHED MIDDAY ROBIN LOST the fight not to doze off on the latter part of the ferry trip. Through sticky eyes he remembered that after the all-night drive he'd neglected to get any sleep. It was all he could do to tell the driver where he needed to get to. He supplied an address and nodded off again. When he awoke the truck was silently parked on the grass outside the house and the driver had left the cab.

He dropped out his door to the ground and stumble-strode around the back. The doors were open and the '42's engine starting up. Robin stood aside as the truck edged out and down the ramp. With the '42 parked beside the paved driveway the moving man went to his truck and came back with clipboard and pen. He noted down several numbers and added them up.

Looks like it comes to sixty-two seventy-five, young fella.

Robin dug out his remaining money and counted.

You can leave off the seventy-five cents. The driver tore off a paper and handed it to Robin.

Robin handed a sheaf of bills over and took the paper as he pulled coins out of the side pocket of his jeans. I'm sure glad you could do this today. Here's the seventy-five cents.

You're a perfect gentleman. Hope you had a good sleep.

I'm feeling awful tired of travelling all of a sudden.

Heh heh. You are one oddball kid. The man's expression firmed into something serious. Is any part of that story you told me true?

Some.

Ha ha. The driver said no more as he stepped away and loaded the ramp. Watching the five-ton recede down the street Robin was surprised at how woozy he was. He decided not to try to gather his things but just proceeded up the walkway to see who was home. He wondered if he should ring the doorbell or simply walk on in. Then the door flung open and his mother hugged him so tightly into the puffy shoulders of her dress that he could say nothing.

Oh my goodness!

He eased his face to one side. Mom.

Where have you been? We were worried sick.

Mom ... He reared back with her arms still about him. I was okay.

I saw you coming up the walk I thought you were a ghost. She stood back and looked him over. You're bigger and your face has gotten so ... Then tears. Oh my goodness. Oh my goodness.

Mom. He eased himself and his mother through the door and into the living room. I'm really tired. I just want to go to bed.

What have you been doing? How did you get here?

That's part of it, Mom. I have to get you to move the car out of the garage.

What? Whyever for?

I need to put my truck in there.

Your truck?

Yes. I drove it here. Or most of the way. It's a long story.

She sank onto the couch and stared at him with wide reddened eyes. Oh my heavens.

It's no big deal, Mom. I'll move it. Where are the keys?

Robin managed to replace the late-model sedan in the garage with the languishing '42 and closed the door on it. He then slept sixteen hours in his old bed. For a few seconds wakening he barely remembered where he was and how he had gotten there. Whether by intention or otherwise his mother lured him from bed by the aroma of breakfast being cooked and he forwent a shower in favour of joining her in the kitchen and partaking of his favourite; French toast with plum jam and scrambled eggs with catsup and coffee.

Your brother wanted to say hello but he had to leave for work.

Oh. Darn. I guess I was asleep when he got in last night.

He had a soccer game.

How's he doing?

She let the question hang just long enough for him to understand it was important to her that he had asked it. Fine.

Good.

He wonders as I do what you were doing driving an old truck across the country. But he's glad as I am that you're back. And just in time for your birthday.

Oh. Yeah.

We missed your other ones.

That's okay.

It'll be so nice to have you here for this one.

It's no big deal.

She turned to him with egg flipper in hand. Things will be fine from now on.

Where's Dad?

Nobody knows for sure. She wiped her hands on a tea towel and glanced out the kitchen window. Last we heard he was headed for Long Beach.

Robin stopped chewing and spoke to her back. Does he have the Airstream?

As far as we know.

What does he —

He's doing what he wants. She turned with an anger-powered abruptness. Maybe someday he'll let us in on it. But for now he's his own man.

Does he send money?

He left as much as we need. Almost all of it from his father's land. I don't know. He's got some kind of philosophy now. He doesn't need anything.

So you're okay?

I invested it. There's enough to send you and Sebastian to school and for me to live on as long as I want to live.

Don't talk like that, Mom.

Well. It isn't the best way to be.

He'll be okay. I'm going out to see him.

But sweetie. School starts in four days.

I'll be here.

She sat at the table and wiped her hands. Tell me what happened. We got the call about Jim Scott the day after he died but nobody could tell us where you were.

Was it Cullen that called?

Yes I think that was who it was.

Good. He'll make sure to get the crop in.

Won't you tell me what happened? Why didn't they put you on a plane? Or get you a train ticket?

Okay Mom I'll tell you ...

Concocting in his mind a carefully edited daily narrative Robin devoured the last of the French toast and began to speak. From the time he loaded the '42 with all that he needed and pulled out of the farmyard — leaving out a certain amorous interlude and then a drug-infused violence scene — to the sleepy ending in front of the house with the truck safely secreted inside a moving truck, his mother listened. The telling took nearly an hour and several refills of coffee. When finished he got up and poured still more.

You never used to drink so much coffee. And black too. Come to think of it you never used to drink coffee at all.

I was twelve, Mom. On the farm you get used to it right away.

And now you're turning sixteen and acting like a middle-aged man. Drifting from place to place. Driving an old truck.

Don't worry, Mom. I won't use it around here. At least not until I get a licence.

But in the meantime you've got this vehicle, which somebody owns, parked in our garage with the door closed like it's a secret.

I own it.

How can you own it?

I just do. You can look at the papers.

Is it legal for a boy to own a vehicle he's not old enough to drive?

It was legal for me on the farm.

You know what I'm talking about, Robin.

Yes, Mom.

I'm going to have to get some advice about it.

Just leave it. It's okay.

I might call Mr. Parker.

Who's that?

Our insurance man. He'll know what to do.

You don't have to, Mom.

What if it's reported stolen?

I told you I own it. Robin tried not to note the pained expression on his mother's face and the way she twisted the strings of her apron in her hands. Everything's okay. Okay?

When I think of you driving that thing a thousand miles across the country ... anything could have happened.

Nothing did.

Oh. I don't know. She looked at him in a way he wished she would not but knew he would have to endure. You've changed. It's not just the few years you were away. There's something different in your face.

They stood square to each other for a time, wordless. Ultimately it all came to a long hug and a gentle sob from his mother.

It's okay, Mom.

I'm so glad you're home.

I am too.

You should just relax. Take some time before school starts and have fun.

I'm going to head to the beach today I think.

Good. Sebastian will be home for dinner.

It'll be good to see him.

He's working at the village garage if you want to drop in on him.

I might.

His bike is in the garden shed. I'm sure you'd be welcome to use it.

I will.

He was glad to shower and find clean clothes but nothing of his old wardrobe came close to a proper fit. His mother threw him slacks and a shirt of his father's. He bound his right ankle with an elastic band so that the bicycle chain would not soil the cuff of the pants as he wheeled into the business centre of the tiny town. His route avoided the garage and any possibility of running into his brother.

The bank was closed for lunch so he had to wait on the sidewalk and window shop for ten minutes. Then he went in and withdrew all that remained in the savings account he had built back when he'd had a paper route. He folded the forty-six dollars and stuck them in a front pocket and took the loose change across the street to the café to sit at the counter and sip a root beer float. No one recognized him and he saw few he could remember save for the waitress who still knew before he spoke what it was that he would order.

After that he wheeled over past the train station and across the tracks to head down the big hill beside the wide veranda of the Qualicum Beach Hotel, its Edwardian dormers nodding across the golf course to the sea below. Across empty lots with narrow passage through trees and scrub and down a precipitous side road astride the last cliff to the beach he whizzed without pedalling. The salt breeze hit his face. He threw down the bike and ran over the sand, shucking shirt and pants down to the trunks he had on and flung himself into the rolling surf.

That evening he set the dinner table while his mother cooked. His brother appeared in mechanic's coveralls and a brown paper–wrapped package in his hands.

Hey.

Robin turned to Sebastian and smiled. Hey.

So you're back, eh?

Looks like it.

Here. Sebastian stepped forward and held the package to Robin. It's your birthday. Right?

Tomorrow.

Well. Close enough.

Sure. Robin took the present and was surprised at its weight.

Sorry I missed the last couple.

Not your fault. Sorry I missed yours.

It's so good to have both of you under one roof again.

Aw, Mom.

It's good to be back on the island. The beach was great. You get used to the dry land and you kind of get to like it. But there's nothing like walking with sand under your feet.

You were born here, dear. It will always be special to you.

Hey, why don't you open that? Sorry it's not wrapped.

Okay. Robin hefted the box to his lap and pulled at the loosely taped paper bag wrapping to reveal the crimson colouring of a metal tool box. Wow.

Mom called me about you getting ripped off. They were selling these down at the station. I get an employee discount.

It's just what I need.

I figured. I took a look in the garage. That's some crazy wheels you got.

Not crazy at all if you come from where I've been. Just plain old everyday transportation.

Well. I don't know how you got it here but it'll be cool to ride around in when you get your licence.

Sure will.

After dinner they sat around.

Sebastian opened the new tool kit and rummaged through the various sockets, ratchets, and screwdriver bits. Maybe next year I'll buy a truck too.

Robin smiled. A couple more years and maybe you could. With your gas jockey wages. How much are you making?

Oh not enough to save much. It's just a summer job and I'm not even an official employee. They get me to clean up and do the basic stuff. It all ends next week but I might get to work weekends if school isn't too much for me.

School is the most important thing.

Yes, Mom.

Gee I had a conversation something like this way up in the mountains a few days ago. It's like a broken record.

Just you make sure you settle down and do well in Grade Ten.

Don't you worry, Mom.

All she does is worry.

You boys know what I worry about and I don't have to apologize for it.

You sure don't, Mom. You sure don't.

These words haunted Robin as he nevertheless composed the midnight note that he pinned to her favourite apron and stole out the side door while the house was asleep.

• • •

He knew to slow-pull the wide folding garage door up so as not to create noise. To ensure quiet he oiled the hinges and runners. He'd backed the '42 into the garage for this kind of escape, sliding the key in and turning the ignition and pulling the stick shift into neutral. With the driver's door open, a hard push, and a leap behind the wheel, the truck took to the driveway incline. He waited for maximum forward movement down the street before dropping in the clutch and giving it just enough choke to catch and steer throbbingly to the corner and away.

The town in this wee hour was quiet as expected but the lone RCMP patrol would be interested in him if sighted. He took care to go the most direct route out of the populated places and within minutes was through a canopy of evergreens almost covering the road west toward the Beaufort mountain range. By recall he was dependent upon one late-night gas stop on this route. He calculated by the wavering fuel needle that he had about enough to get there. No more than three cars were met oncoming and no one appeared ahead or behind as he wheeled into the siding to where a single light shone over the gas pump beside a general store. The bing of the signal wire in the silence of the night was audible even over the rumble of the '42's straight six cylinders.

About ten seconds went by before a light came on in the store. A scratching-headed man in coveralls emerged from the garage and strode into his headlight beams. Then he was at Robin's side with bleary eyes not saying a word.

Fill 'er up.

The silent man went about his assignment. Robin closely monitored the gas counter on the pump and selected as near to correct an amount as he could to meet the total. In the end he gave three dollars for a two-dollar and eighty-five cent sale and the man grunted when his young customer waved off the offer of fifteen cents' change. As Robin pulled away he reflected that in the whole transaction the man had scarcely glanced at him. The dark road was welcoming now that he knew he had enough gas to get where he was going. The fresh night air coming through the half-open window braced him.

After a flat stretch past dairy farms and a gravel pit the road spiralled into a series of hill-climbs that the truck took well. Robin seldom had to gear down. Then he was twisting and turning alongside Cameron Lake with rock overhangs and near hairpin swerves along scant siding that would not hold much back in the case of a skid or loss of control. He knew of travellers who had gone into the lake and had to swim for it with the terrible sense that the depth of the water ensured their vehicles would never be seen again.

Past the lake there was a turn-off for tourists to see and walk among some of the largest trees in the world but in the head-light tunnel he could only concentrate on the negotiation of the serious curves and attenuation of his speed. At a point near the end of the grove he detected up forward a flash of red. Then nothing for a few seconds. Then red again. He rolled slower and tried to think as taillights from more than one car came into consistent view. In another five seconds he comprehended that a car was parked partially off the road and another with rear lights still burning was off to the side and accordioned up against an immense Douglas Fir.

He rolled still slower and was contemplating going past when a dark-clothed man strode to the middle of the road and held up authoritative arms. There was nothing to do but stop. As the man approached he noted wild eyes.

You can't ever move them or they're dead. As soon as you move them they're dead.

Robin struggled to catch up with the distraught man's assertions. All he could come up with over the rumble of the engine was: Uh …

When I die they're going to put me in a box. A plain wood box. None of this fancy casket expense for me.

Through the semi-dark and the dome light of the truck he had flipped on during this last *non sequitur* Robin could see that the man was ruddy-faced and wore a clerical collar. Uh …

The man stepped back and motioned for him to park the truck ahead of the car. He followed as Robin did just this.

Stepping to the road Robin debated whether to leave lights on and risk running down the battery. Luckily he located his flashlight where it had escaped theft behind the seat. He pushed the truck's lights off as he fingered the flashlight switch on to illuminate the man standing nearby. Before he could think of something to say, lights came up from behind them and a brapp-brapping muscle car slowed in from the Port Alberni direction. A window rolled down. Hey. Need help? What's going on?

Robin and the reverend approached the car as it idled loudly in the middle of the highway. There's people hurt down there. The clerical man pointed toward the crashed car and spoke with an oratorial authority. Can you run for help?

Well sure but … is it bad?

Bad enough for God to have forsaken all who travelled in that vehicle there, friend.

Um … Robin had to yell above the souped-up roar. I just came through from Qualicum. Whiskey Creek store is open.

It might be faster to go back to Alberni.

Whichever you think.

Should we take him in ourselves? I got the backseat free.

The reverend shoved his face fully into the young man's window and bellowed his opinion: When you move them you kill them!

Is that so? The driver shifted his car into gear. I'll phone for help at Whiskey Creek. Likely the ambulance from Port will come.

Okay.

Once the car was gone nearly the only luminance was from Robin's flashlight. There was a residual headlight reflection from the trees that came from what he assumed was the reverend's car. He watched him open a back door of the sedan and pull out a blanket.

Go make the young man comfortable. He pointed to the steaming wreck. I'll flag help if it will come to us.

Oh. Okay.

Robin took the blanket and turned toward the ditch. Before he got there he saw that he'd have to take care getting down to the car due to a deep side-cut in the road between the tarmac and where the tree line began. As he neared the open driver's door a moaning he thought he'd heard became more clear. He trained the light on a teenager a few years older than he sit-standing half in and half out of the crumpled front. The car looked to be a late-model Rambler station wagon though in the gloom and through the damage he could not be sure.

The teen grimaced and tried to move. My back.

Don't move. Here. Robin tossed the blanket over the youth and tucked it around his torso. We sent for help. Just relax.

Where's Julie?

Julie? There was somebody with you?

Julie … He realized the youth was not fully conscious and was gazing vacantly off into the forest darkness as if expecting to see someone emerge.

Robin stepped to the rear and shone his light into the closed window of the backseat and could see little in the reflection. He pried opened the door and had to lean back and yard on it to get a wide enough gap. A smell hit him with familiarity despite the uniqueness of the circumstances and it took seconds for him to place it. Beer. Once identified he understood that the whole interior of the car reeked and was in fact wet with sudsy brew and glinting with amber glass fragments. In the beam of his light he could see a girl of about sixteen lying on her side between the slick wet seat and the front seatback. She whimpered softly.

I can't move.

Don't try. We sent for help.

I can't move.

Don't.

I can't feel anything.

Oh …

While he rued the feeling of having nothing to say to someone so needing of solace the sound of thrashing and the driver
repeating the name of Julie Julie Julie was beginning to un-
nerve him. The reverend clambered aside. Good. You found the
alive one. Don't move her.

I won't.

Don't go to the front.

Huh?

She is to heaven or to hell or to nothing if you prefer.
Depending on what sacred thing you believe. Where dogs and
geckos go. Or perhaps she's a saint at the third hand of God.

Damn it. I'm sorry sir but what you're saying doesn't make
sense and it's no help right now. You say there's another one?

If Robin hadn't been holding the flashlight on the reverend's face he would not have seen what he instantly regretted
seeing. The man's features were twisted into a mask of utter
suffering. Though slight, his stumble onto Robin's shoulder for
support shocked him with its weight and boney discomfort.
The reverend put his mouth to Robin's ear: Through the windshield my young friend.

I didn't see any …

But he knew he hadn't looked far after covering the driver
with the blanket. He stepped around the reverend and struggled through the underbrush to the front of the car. The area
was still ashroud with steam up from the compacted radiator.
One of the Rambler's headlights was still functioning but
skewed aside to light an adjacent tree and not the massive speci-
men the car had slammed into.

At first he could see nothing but the aftermath of metallic mayhem. The crumpled hood was raised and folded and the
bumper had flung itself in a bracelet of chrome around the tree
trunk. The impact had raised the fenders to bloom as jagged

barriers along each side of the front end so as to prevent full sight
of the destruction. He moved around one threatening cluster of
sharp shards and pointed the light to the join of car and tree.
He saw a department store mannequin's foot with pedal-pusher
pant-leg askew lying incongruously with other parts amid a bed
of diamonds on the remains of the hood and then understood
that the leg was attached to the rest of the assembly and this was
actually a human girl and was likely named Julie.

Such was the bizarre posture of the body that he scarcely
believed it organic. The arms were at odd angles off the torso
and bent and broken in places unimaginable. The head was
twisted upon the neck so radically he wondered that it had
remained attached. Glinting shards of safety glass adorned the
body and the general site.

Robin tried to ignore the wreath of blood that was her hair
as he leaned across the wreckage. An odd warmth rose into
his body, penetrating in a way that confused him in its combination of pity and attraction. He craned his head in close to
see if her face was intact. In some strange way he was gratified
that it was and as he waved the light her eyes opened and made
contact with his. If they had not been so lovely and accepting
he might have recoiled stumbling. But they focused on his and
widened with some kind of recognition that he knew must be
general or mistaken or reflexive. With a mystified sigh she uttered in a voice pleasant as water over ornamental stones a word
that he nearly missed due to its prosaic familiarity: Gosh …

The word left her lips in such a resigned way and the tone
of her look into his face suggested such here-to-stay sweetness
that his heart flew at the idea she might live. Gosh yourself.
Are you going to hang on with us so we can get you some help?

Even as he uttered the final word of this sentence the
eyes dulled and tension flagged throughout her body. Robin

staggered back. Tears leapt to his eyes and a revulsion rose so sudden and violent he nearly could not turn away in time to vomit in a stream against the offended tree.

Stumbling up from the ditch spitting and tearful he saw that other cars had stopped, one of them nearly boxing in the '42. With no further thought to stay and an encroaching knowledge that the police would be arriving soon he strode past standing figures to slide into the cab, gulp a mouthful of water and spit to the pavement, then start up and carefully steer onto the highway.

From there it was a long serious climb up a swerving incline upon which he eventually had to shift down to first gear. The tears in his eyes made driving even at his slow rate up the hill a challenge and he was at least glad he'd been over this road many times as a passenger and knew it well. The lug took ten minutes or so and the roar of the truck's willing engine combined with a gentler breeze through the night mountain forest all around slowly calmed him sufficient to stop weeping. He one-hand gripped the wheel hard to wipe his face. Flashing lights appeared ahead and disappeared and then came at him full on as first an ambulance and then the police screamed over the mountain. At the summit he eased out of gear and on the slight decline let the truck coast off some of the heat it had accumulated. Then there was a radical downhill brake and steer session the touchiness of which in the dark nearly took his mind off what he knew was the worst thing he had ever been part of. Rumbling down the side of Mount Arrowsmith he resolved never to stop at an accident scene again.

He was nevertheless comforted in his freedom. He was never so glad to have sufficient fuel and time to just drive and drive. Deftly navigating through the lit streets of Alberni in the two a.m. night was uneventful but the concentration of zooming through an urban area with more than one traffic signal to obey gave him welcome purpose and occupation of mind. Hours into the night, mile turned into many miles turned into timeless headlong flight past lakeside shore roads and mountain switchbacks and gravel gullies on dust-spewing grades. He noticed the still-on flashlight rolling on the seat beside him. The dullness of the beam said he'd have to get new batteries soon. He switched it off.

He sensed also that in the heaviness of the air and columns of conical light his headlamps created there was a particulate irregularity ahead. A scent of woodsmoke suggested a thousand fireplaces going at a time. At a high point aside Sproat Lake he noted a crimson glow on a horizon well before any sunlight would be expected. Forest fire.

Along the lapping lake the smoke began to collect. Though keen to keep going, he slowly understood it was likely that he might have to stop and reconsider.

Out past the last great arm of vast lake water the glow in the sky positively shone. He rounded a bend and rolled direct up to a barrier of two RCMP cruisers nosed together. An officer stood in the road holding out a stop hand. It was too late to pretend he might casually park by the side among the other vehicles he now noticed scattered about. Robin braked slow and half-turned his face only sufficient so that in the darkness his youth might be masked.

You can't go through.

Okay …

Pull over and get up to the fire unit. I have to detain you for emergency firefighting. They need every man they can get.

Over there?

Anywhere. Just get your truck out of the way. You'll be helping the hill crew. Hope you brought work boots. The constable trained his flashlight beam to where Robin was to park.

With mixed pleasure and alarm Robin pulled away and edged the '42 well off the roadway to a side space between a late-model sedan and a boxy logging transport. Before he could open his door a grizzled man appeared and proffered a metal hard hat similar to the dented and stained one he was wearing. You'll need this right away. Wind is changing.

Uh ... Robin pulled his farm straw off and replaced it with the safety topper. He stepped from the '42.

Are you a conscript, son? Or did you sign on?

They stopped me ... Robin pointed to the police in the road now standing by the light of their cars regarding him at the distance with stern expressions ... and told me what to do.

Then you're a conscript. Sorry about that. Don't know how long we'll need you but we sure do need you. The man trained a flashlight downward. How's your footwear?

Uh ...

As they spoke crimson cinders began to rain about them and the difficulty in breathing became acute. The man pulled a pair of heavy work gloves from an over-shoulder bag and handed them to Robin. He nodded to the '42. You better roll those windows up. No telling what's coming.

Robin did as instructed and kicked the side of the box to show the man that his boots would likely suffice for the purposes it looked like they would be put to.

Okay come on. My name's Jack. What's yours?

Robin.

Well Robin you've got yourself into a tough one here.

What am I supposed to do?

You'll see. They crossed what to Robin looked like an impenetrable bush line on the high side of the road and climbed steep and rough through the trees. At a level clearing a group of men milled about in the glow of a dozen flickering torches, their hard hats emitting a glinting strobe. There were several distinct collections of personnel. The din of electric generators and growling power saws up to the high side made conversation a shouting affair.

Jack leaned close to Robin's ear and pointed to a pile of gear. Grab a shovel! And wait for me over there. He nodded toward the start of a dark pathway leading upward where many men were assembled and brandishing what looked like a grand variety of gardening tools. You're on firebreak duty.

Waiting with the others Robin was issued a web-slung water bottle and a packet of what he assumed would be some kind of food. After ten minutes of standing around in the coughing atmosphere Jack came around with still more shovel- and Pulaski-bearing men. He trained his flashlight in the intended direction and wordlessly proceeded on up the dark path. Everyone followed.

The incline was steep but the worst part for Robin was the frequent necessity to either climb over massive fallen trunks or squirm under them. He took care not to snag himself too nastily on the barbs and sticks and scratching points. In half an hour the corps was fully mouth-breathing and sodden with effort. Eventually they arrived at a work site with swarms of men digging and pickaxing at the ground along a near invisible line through the fire-lit forest up the hillside. Farther up, the flickering and sometimes flaring yellow-orange rage of the proximate inferno issued a spooky sound. With few words the new crew set to continue the clearing work of the group they'd come to relieve.

Robin saw the method immediately. They were to swipe clean of wood and underbrush as wide and fuelless a gap through the trees as could be managed to stop the breeze-led march of the smoke-belch crackle-mad conflagration that now could be seen and heard across the mountainside.

It was clear the fire was approaching.

Git to 'er boys!

Robin was unsure that Jack actually called this exhortation and considered that he imagined it as he among the others flung to the task. The heat and dust rose with their effort and the incidence of coughing became the ambient sound. Hours passed. Beside them in the trees there was a machine sound that Robin identified as pumps and related equipment. As he worked, one note of the assembled rumblings gave him pause. He tried, in the unseen smoke-choking hot air, to allow himself to empty into sheer labour and forget any mechanical thing that might nag him. But after another hour or so as the crew worked farther up the slope and he positioned closer to the roaring over-stress of the machinery he turned aside as Jack stumbled down the line and shouted to be heard.

What?

Mixture!

What?

Robin straightened and put his mouth to the man's ear. The mixture. I think that pump motor there is going to burn out if the fuel mix isn't adjusted.

You mean the supply-line hose? Jack looked quizzical and then glanced to where the unit was barely visible in the gloom and then back at Robin. You sure?

Nope. But I'd take a look at it anyway.

Well … Jack straightened and gestured Robin away from the digging line. Show me.

They stumbled through broken undergrowth to where a line of canvas hose led into the near-coughing relay machine and then upward to another whose motorized voice in the near distance sounded much steadier. The pump sat on a mound of cut lumber and discarded fuel cans and the off-colour exhaust of it combined with the smoke in the air had both of them gagging.

Over the noise Jack had to yell. Is this the one you think needs changing?

Robin pulled off his gloves. Yeah. He leaned near and touched the top of the carburetor housing.

Careful. Jack waved his hand. It'll be hot.

Not this part. Shouldn't be.

Oh. You know these things?

Some. Robin looked around. Are there any tools?

Pump boss patrols up and down the hill to keep these things going. He's got what tools he needs.

Even a screwdriver. Or a dime.

Jack dug in his dungarees. Here's ten cents.

Robin yanked off what he knew would likely be a snap-on covering over the fuel line and related components and in Jack's flashlight beam immediately saw the adjustment slot. He reached in with the coin and varied the mixture plug a quarter turn. The motor coughed deep and threatened to stall. Robin immediately wristed in the other direction and the engine's note calmed audibly. He let it run for a moment before turning the screw a slight bit farther. The motor settled to a steady thrum that Jack visibly heard and whose happy grin and nodding approval Robin received with unexpected gratitude.

Good job, my boy.

No big deal. I was afraid maybe the jets were fouled. That would have been big trouble.

The jets eh? You know this stuff.

Robin replaced the cover and snapped it into place. I worked around a lot of machinery.

Well hell, young fella. I'll put you on mechanic duty. We're trying to get a D8 CAT going down the hill. Think you can help?

Maybe. I worked on some diesel.

They're having hydraulics trouble is what I'm told.

I know hydraulics.

Jack straightened and pointed to the cleared track. You go down near as far as the lake. It's a good walk. Tell 'em I sent ya. You might stop at the depot and see if they can spare you some tools and any more fuel they might have.

Okay.

Gimme that shovel.

Robin handed it over.

Get on down there. I'll radio that you're coming. Be careful.

Here's your dime. Robin held it out.

Keep it. You're worth the money.

Both laughed.

On his way Robin stopped twice more to fine-tune hot-roaring pumper relay units. At the clearing he readily received a tool kit and jerry can of diesel oil and replenished his water bottle. A quick glance crossing the road let him be assured that the '42 stood unmolested where he'd parked it. Then it was down farther through the woods past sweaty crews of hose men hooking up and transferring great weights of high-pressure double-jacket stock and moiling about with knock-end rocker couplings and pin lugs to string out the attack lines.

After a half hour of careful picking over the narrow trail down toward the water he came upon a duo tinkering atop a silent crawler bulldozer. They took notice of him immediately and climbed down. Hey did you get the stuff we asked for?

Any spare water? I'm out.

Robin proffered the tool box. If this is it then I guess I did.

One man took the tools and opened the lid. Ah yeah here it is. He gripped a wrench. Female swivel nut grabber for that bunged-up hexagonal. Finally.

Gimme a drink, will you. The other man took Robin's newly filled water bottle and took a long awkward swallow before Robin could whip the strap from around his neck. Their mutual contortions in accomplishing this went completely unnoticed by the drinker's serious-faced tool-wielding partner.

Both men then returned to perches on the massive tooth-footed vehicle.

Do you know the names of stuff? The wrenchman called down to Robin through a now-audible wind and the distant pop and sizzle of the fire. Can you hand us up what we need when we need it?

Sure.

Okay. Grab that bucket. We're gonna open up this baby and we can't spare any more fluid.

Robin did as instructed and watched as the men dealt efficiently with what looked to him to be a marred connection at one end of a hydraulic line that in the rising light reminded him of a job he'd assisted on the prairie not so long ago but now seemed a separate lifetime.

Come on up and hold this.

Robin scrambled to see what was required and saw that he would be the assistant to the cleanup phase of what had been a major in-the-field repair.

As they completed the task Jack trotted down the hill and leaned with a hand on the scarred metal blade of the machine to peer at the progress being made. You guys done up there?

Just about.

Okay. Quick as you can. Up the track the fellows made for you.

That's a fifty-degree grade. Maybe more.

Do it backward. She'll make it.

Says you.

No other way.

We'll try.

Take the kid with you. Jack smiled. He's good luck.

Both men looked up from their work and gave Robin a gaze they'd been heretofore too busy to make. Their expressions were weighty to the point that all he could do was meet their eyes momentarily and then stare down at the remainder of the hydraulics job.

Jack turned and began a grunting climb back up the mountainside. One of the men swung up into the wire-cage cockpit and monkeyed with levers and switches before a gout of blue smoke issued from the piping exhaust and the air was full of still more ear-bending sound. Robin helped the other man finish gathering the tools and clambered with him into the cockpit to stand behind the operator who when all was clear raised the ten-foot-wide blade a few feet in the air and pushed the transmission into reverse with a seismic clunk.

It became immediately clear that the job of passenger on a reversing CAT was to survey the ground to be covered and advise the back-facing driver of anything too big to overcome or depression too low. Speed was necessary. The two observers kept as careful a watch as could be managed within the tossing case by bar-holds they were forced to grip with both hands as the machine bucked and yawed on its growling way up the incline. At times along the thousand-or-so-yard course the smoke was so thick they were obliged to advise the driver to slow to be sure there were no lingering workers in the giant Caterpillar's path. Most of the time and through the nearly one hour it took to scale the slope there was little but half-upended stumps and discarded trunks littering the way. At critical times the machine listed so that the standing crew was forced to grip hard and lean ahead to add whatever puny purchase their weight might lend to keeping the thirty-ton mass properly clung upon the incline. The driver had several times to flick down the trailing blade into the seething dust to stabilize.

As full-sun daylight granted the hillside more shape and texture the bulldozer broke through a level of air at least fresh and certainly cooler. Looking about them the men saw that they had reached the summit and a resting work crew was encamped by a pond in a scrub forest. Sandwiches were in evidence and there was a smell of coffee.

The three CAT riders exhaled in unison as they arrived on a rare level spot and the driver moved to shut down for at least as much time as it would take to wolf a bite and gulp a cup. Before that could happen a man with a different colour hard hat hurried up. Thank Christ you guys finally got here.

You're welcome. The driver spoke with fingers lingering over the kill switch. What's for breakfast?

Eat on the run, boys. The man swung a canvas bag into the cab that landed at Robin's feet then handed up a large thermos and a three-gallon water jug. Get that rig scraping down the hill right now. Morning wind is due any time and we're never sure which direction. He pointed down a side of the mountain they had not been facing and it was clear then to the bulldozer crew that their down-route might well be a flame tour of great peril. Smoke swirled from old growth evergreens by their full length and even from a considerable distance they could hear the frequent explosive whoosh-crack of individual trees spontaneously igniting. The inferno was clearly advancing on the hard-fought gap cleared by the exhausted spade-men strewn around the clearing.

Without further discussion the driver pushed the CAT into forward gear and eased toward the top of the firebreak. He lowered the blade as they approached and in so doing widened

the space by at least a foot on either side and began also to dig a
top layer of mossy soil and wood-slag waste aside so as to leave
a clear dirt track behind.

This sweeping of a bare dirt forest corridor Robin saw was the
ultimate fire-beating strategy. Their ponderous downhill momen-
tum made immense movements of soil and rock fold into berms
and banks on both sides. Occasional outposts of hose-men stood
spraying the non-fire-side making ready for the advance of the
inevitable flame. Robin and his mate snatched bites of egg sandwich and sips of coffee while trying to prevent being bucked off
the howling machine. They took frequent turns lending vision-
clearing branch removal assistance to the squinting driver.

Though downhill progress was less straining for the machine, because of the wind the crew now contended with
thicker dust in a breath-stopping mix with the ever-increasing
smoke. As they approached mid-hill an extra-savage wave of
heat assaulted them. Robin had been getting used to the extreme temperature but he and his cabmates exchanged grave
glances as an orange tongue shot across their field of vision
a few feet ahead. As they inched ever downward Robin felt
an increasing discomfort over the top of his head. Through
his gloved hand he felt a serious heat come off his metal hat.
Liberal dousings of the drinking water over the face and down
the shirtfronts of the men were only token adaptations to this
new level of torrid. The driver yelled something unintelligible
and yanked a package out from under the instrument panel.
Each man was soon wreathed in a shimmering thermal shield
that turned them into metallic cocoons. They glimmered in the
beams of sunlight seeping through the dusty smoke and the
more frequent glarings of flame nearby.

Occasional moments of relief came when passing the hose
companies who would immediately train their misting nozzles

at the machine and the men upon it. But as they moved mid-hill the heat was of a type that at once paradoxically improved air quality but raised the surface temperature of the metal they depended upon to points impossible to touch even with heavy glove protection.

Robin wondered at what stage he would lose his grip on calm and leap running from the fire. At the worst moment the two crew huddled in the lee of the driver, away from the fire side as he furiously drove the carving blade into the earth and downward toward a lakeside that mercifully now could briefly be seen through the live treetops and ghosting flame.

Robin took an opportunity to glance back on their progress and saw that the widened and deepened track their effort yielded was indeed helping corral the fire. As they passed by, the hose men were stepping into the gap and firing their nozzles into the furnace. Greasy steam-smoke and kicked-up cinders of fuming fir bark nearly obscured their work.

Turning back to face ahead Robin was startled by the sight of an enormous airplane heading straight for the hill they were on, seemingly to the very spot they occupied. For a millisecond the panic of imminent oblivion took away breath and forced a bowel-clenching effort. As the giant white-and-red-painted roaring bird came closer its flight path elevated such that it seemed to Robin they might be spared instant death but that the crew of the plane was nevertheless doomed to slam into the mountainside above them. He could see the headphone-wearing pilots through their windshield and marvelled at their daring. Then a massive white descended upon all. Robin felt it as a most pleasing mist on his flaring face and understood that they were being aided in the fight by a Mars water bomber. He'd read about them. And now amid the momentary heat relief and the further amelioration of the forest fire he knew about them. He heard no impact as the freighter shadowed past and roared over the hill crest out of sight.

They had passed mid-point. Robin could see now that their goal was a beach. It gleamed at the bottom of the hill more and more often as the CAT sometimes bounced jauntily on its way. As they emerged from the worst of the flying combusted pine needles and fuming cedar fronds the driver edged up the throttle and it seemed only a few more minutes before they emerged from dense forest onto a white sand ribbon of placid shoreline.

Ignoring the collection of men standing about and the set-up of food and water thereabouts all members of the bulldozer mission leapt off the machine as a unit and bounded into the lake. Hard hat metal sizzled on contact. Men and boy sighed in the joyous coolness and floated face down for as long as lung capacity would allow.

The milling cadre drinking from canteens and chomping hot sandwiches took little or no notice of the bathers but some expressed concern that the idled CAT remained on the beach still beating its mighty diesel heart. Someone stepped up to the cab and deftly switched off the fuel supply.

As breathing became imperative Robin slowly rolled to gaze skyward and was taken by the stark unblemished blue of the sky. With ears below water he enjoyed the quiet. The coolness all about him was a revelation of comfort. He was descending toward sleep when a gag for watery breath woke him fully and prompted an exit. Standing a-drip in the sun he was glad to receive a hot bacon-and-egg sandwich and steaming coffee. A general mutter existed among the standing and sitting cohort that did not particularly include him so Robin sought out and consumed two more sandwiches and three more cups of coffee.

As a contingent gathered gear and prepared to move back up the mountain he found a store of blankets and realized a collection of foam mattresses were arranged in rows just inside the forest. He pulled a couple of covers from the pile and found the farthest-most tablet among the trees. After pulling sodden clothes off and hanging them on branches he curled into a fetal crescent and immediately lost consciousness.

Such was the state of his physical exhaustion and the hours gone without sleep and the mental toll taken by the lifetimes of experience between the time he'd left his mother's protection and his arrival at the end of this grand forest fire effort that Robin slept for an unbroken span of fourteen hours.

Lurching alive in complete darkness he first wondered if the effect of all this adventure had been an unjust blindness. He rubbed his face and crept with the blankets around him up into a forehead-to-knees crouch. Listening close he detected a trend of movement and soft voice and following these cues he did eventually see by campstove glow and flashlight flicker that there were others around and the food and coffee operation was still in motion. All around him were animalistic sounds he soon understood to be the snoring of an unknown number of men.

He was gratified to find his clothes dry and quickly dressed and made for the row of temporary outhouses illuminated by a thin row of glow strips. Afterward he strolled to the lake and washed his face and hands. At the cookstove two men sat tending a boiling pot of water and large table full of hamburger buns.

Howdy there. Feel like a burger?

Sure do. What time is it?

Huh … The man not cooking flashed a light to his wrist. Just after one a.m.

Thanks. I sure slept a long time.

What crew are you?

I was on that Caterpillar.

Oh yeah? Well you lost your ride. They moved out late afternoon.

Well. I wasn't on steady anyway. Robin looked around and could see much more now that his eyes were accustomed to the varied dark. Where's the fire now?

Moved over the mountain. The man pointed up the track and away. That direction. You get finished here they'll need you on firebreak crew down the other side.

Oh.

Robin accepted two hamburger buns with two patties on each and doused them with liberal coats of mustard and catsup. He found a picnic table to sit at and carefully ate. Despite the necessity of thinking through his next move he could not get over the deliciousness of this meal. Never in memory had he had such a scrumptious repast. He shook his head and wondered if he was not still asleep.

But as he consumed the last bite a mental chill overtook and an immediate imperative to get moving seized him. Without further words to anyone he tossed the paper plate he'd been eating off into a garbage can and stepped into darkness. He knew the route upward and his eyes gathered just enough starlight to guide him among the stumps and slag.

For a good few minutes he carefully picked his way upward and then stepped onto the level gravel interruption he knew would be the road.

As he stood looking both ways up and down the blackened forest hallway, shadows appeared to the west before a winking headlight. He stepped into the bush as the car sped past. For a moment the significance of its direction did not register to him but then the revelation that it had come from the direction he desired hit his brain. As the dust settled in the car's wake he understood that the road west was no longer closed.

He walked back toward where he'd been stopped a day ago. To one side down the mountain there was only blackness and up the other the glow of the now-distant fire made the sky an amber burnished canvas.

In a few minutes he rounded a bend and saw the faint glint of the '42's distinctive cab outlines amid the collection of vehicles and lights near the firefighters' depot. Police were nowhere in sight but activity audibly continued in the camp. He stepped to his truck expecting a call from someone somewhere and was ever so glad not to receive one. With care he removed his hard hat and placed it soundlessly on a stump.

The feeling of the seat upholstery on his back and legs was a balm and he opted to sit for a moment and enjoy it without even closing the door. Then he reasoned that to make a cleaner escape he would best start the engine and pull into the roadway without lights. This he did with dispatch and was soon down the road far enough with lights on thrilling at the rush of wind in the window. With nothing showing in the rear-view a feeling of release descended upon him such that he had not had since leaving the farm all those eons ago.

• • •

Just before dawn began to tint the sky Robin saw ahead that he was near the end of the westward route. A sign at a three-way intersection offered a choice between Ucluelet and Tofino.

Though the light of a cloudless day was rising behind him he still could not perceive in the gloom across the road and through the woods what he knew would be the Pacific Ocean. Standing at the stop sign alone with the '42 idling he reflected on the dirt-rutted miles covered to attain this juncture. He poked his face out to sniff the breeze for its unmistakable sea-foam flavour. He cut the engine and accepted the low moan of an immense unseen surf. The tone and smell of everything filled him with an unexpected elation.

The silence inspired him to take a look at himself in the rearview. This he did with a hand up on the mirror and the other tilting back his hat to take in the full visage. Little remained of his eyebrows. From side to side a reddish shading spanned his face across eyes and cheeks and nose. His ears gave a rosy glow and felt hot in the fresh morning air. Though essentially uninjured and feeling lucky about it he noted that his fingers were sensitive where they contacted the steering wheel.

Still alone on the road he restarted the truck and pulled a right turn toward where he'd once been set loose to run and play on beaches. The morning air was nearly too chill so he cranked the window up to just an inch or so to let the new air swirl about. He spied a turnoff and took a left into a car-crowded lane down to a driftwood barricade. Licence plates of every North American location flashed by: Oregon, Ontario, Nevada, Arizona, Alberta, New York … It buttressed his confidence that parking the '42 with its Saskatchewan tags amid this menagerie of disparate origins would not attract particular attention. He pulled it into a nose-in space close to the beach, rolled the windows up, and locked the doors.

He emerged from the narrow bushy portal out onto a wide sand spread where a stronger blast of ocean wind with mist moved his hair around. Everywhere in both directions there were camping configurations of all manner ranging from lean-to tents against bicycles to elaborate tarpaulin shore-steads with beach rock patios and fire pits with tastefully arranged Adirondack chairs. Though barely yet six a.m. there were people moving about in the distance and closer but the sparse distribution of the few humans in this immense space made it seem like he was standing alone. Once sated by the exhilaration of the pure oxygen and the gull cries and the sand below his boots he strode back.

The '42 lugged up the dusty hill back to the main road and as casual traffic whizzed by in both directions he remembered with a mental lurch that in the now-brilliant sunshine of day he was identifiably who he was once more, no longer camouflaged by the cloak of nighttime. He headed briskly down the road toward Tofino. In a few miles there was a large turnoff into a marshy parking lot where varieties of vehicles and camping rigs were either stationed or haphazardly strewn about in no particular organizational structure. He had to carefully thread a route down a maze of narrow lanes to find the wider access to the beach. With fluttering heart he pulled the '42 over a low driftwood-and-gravel berm and rumbled onto the hard dry sand along the tide-sloped shore.

There were more people around now and a fair few cars, trucks, buses, and odd hybrid machines of adapted motorcycle tractor wagon and sidecar varieties on the low dunes. Robin formed in his mind a mental picture of what the Airstream might look like amid the general clutter. He opted to begin patrolling the larger side of the vast beach so turned toward it, keeping watch for shambling pedestrians.

It became immediately clear that the overall tone of the place made it unlikely he would attract the attention of authorities. In fact the beach's indiscriminate bivouacking and apparent absence of law and order seemed to engender a sense of medieval bacchanal. Everywhere there were scant-clad celebrants of the sun and breeze prancing to unheard melodies. Children ran naked. Adults strolled and drank and chatted casually with everyone they met. A drumbeat pounded somewhere and never went out of earshot.

Amid this rolling festival Robin became mentally enmeshed

in wondrousness. He felt more secure in what he was about than at any time since his tires had left the farm.

It took near a quarter-hour for him to get to the end of the bay. He turned around and started back, taking care to give other vehicles a broad range as there were no lines on the beach or traffic laws of the sand.

Out toward the surf Robin became aware of a particularly large gathering and noted that they were congregated around an antique city bus. As he got nearer a pair of young women peeled away and ran to stand in his path. As he slowed one of them approached his window. Can you help? We're stuck. She pointed to the bus.

Robin came to a full stop and looked over to now see that the wheels of the big lumbering vehicle were sunk nearly to axle depth and that the collection of people all around were pushing while the wheels spun sand to the air.

The tide is coming in! The second woman spoke to him through the passenger window. Can you give us a tow with this thing?

You mean that bus? It's pretty heavy.

We have people. They can push it. You can pull it with your truck, can't you?

He weighed the risks and possible outcomes. It'll have to be lightened. This is only a half-ton. My tires aren't full-traction treads. I'm not sure I can do any good.

Would you try please?

Well ...

Though his reluctance was strong the girl's voice touched a nerve in him and Aldis's and the dying girl's and any female verbal note that had ever entreated him — including his mother's — now tugged at his emotional innards. He gazed at the developing scene around the bus. People were coalescing

into a reverse fire-bucket line to transfer items from the camp-
erized unit to slightly higher sand some yards back. He noted
that the larger swells coming in from Japan were slapping
against the front and would soon reach the rear where even over
the thrum of the '42 he could hear the diesel's desperation roar.

The look of the effluent belching from the back was an alert
also. A jet black that spoke of over-revs and possible fuel con-
tamination and a greasy cloud issuing sporadically from the
low mounted and near sand-choked exhaust pipes.

It looks bad but ... Okay. I'll pull around.

Can you hook it up at the front?

Better I get connected somehow at the rear end. He twirled
the wheel and motored the twenty yards or so to the bus and
then pulled around and backed to within a few feet of where
a phalanx of swimsuited youths were trying to hoist the bus
with sheer brawn.

He hopped from the cab and reached behind the seat for
the heaviest hawser he'd brought along. A man watched him
unwind the coil.

Tell the guy to put it in neutral until I say. Robin spoke as
he knelt on the moist surface and tried to get an idea of the
bus's understructure. He made out towing loops on either side.
Hey. Could you guys lift on a count of three so I can get this
line through the loops? He had to yell over the growling diesel.

A common understanding seemed to flow through the
group and the task of attaching the sinking bus — now fully in
contact with tidewater at the front and occasionally swamped
by the fast rushing wave action at the rear — was urgent.

Tell him to put it in reverse and watch for my hand out the
window. I'll give him a signal when I'm ready to gun it. You
guys lift at the same time, eh.

Right on, man.

He knew that a straight attempt at towing would immediately bury his own drive tires so deep he might never emerge. With this in mind he'd let out as much of the rope as he had so that there would be room for the '42 to accelerate in first gear and develop as much forward haul as he dared to subject to its ancient trailer hitch. He waved to bystanders to clear a path for him. A swell came charging to wet his cuffs and drowned his boots. A groan went up among the volunteer pushers. He slid back behind the wheel and revved the engine. The crowd around gave a cheer.

He backed slightly until almost touching the bus and put out a hand. As a collective shout of "Go Man!" rose he throttled the '42 ahead and nearly out of the gout of stinky smoke that chased him until after thirty feet or so the rope tautened and he had to fend with both hands the forward force acting on his head and body. He was taken aback by the impact but held a foot on the gas enough to keep the wheels spinning. By the rearview he could not see if there had been progress but a check to the side said he was not moving and then the rear end of the '42 sank the foot or so that it would take to bottom on the axle. He backed off the gas.

Hey man we nearly did it. A tie-dyed fellow had come to the cab and leaned close. I think if we coordinate better we can get better purchase. Maybe we should put some people in your truck here to get better traction, eh?

Yeah. Might do it.

He put it in reverse and gently gave it gas. The '42 lurched and then dug in. I'm going to need a push to get out of this hole.

Sure thing man. Hey! Come over and lift this truck out.

A quick organization of helpers soon had the '42 back into position to try again. By now the water was resident at the front of the bus. Waves pushed against it and the general water level sluiced into the open door. At the rear the exhaust burbled through sea water.

Okay we have to get right to it. He called to bystanders. Can somebody ride in the back here and hold on tight?

Four willing participants leapt into the bed and buttressed themselves against the sides and the tailgate. He turned to the hoisters and pushers. Get ready.

We're ready.

Back in the truck he shifted into gear, then stuck out his hand and heard the diesel once more rise up in sound and fume. He gave the '42 all the gas it could take and let out the clutch. The truck bounded ahead.

To rightly manipulate the brute forces involved he summoned all the mechanical insight the prairies had imparted to him and tried with objectivity to assess what the best method might be. Experience in snow conditions and other limited traction messes — not least the gumbo mud show at the beginning of every spring and autumn — had him riding the clutch to a certain extent. It was important to get as much torque while at the same time maximizing grip in a slippery environment. As the tension was drawn up and the lurch forward endured by all in the bed and by the determined driver and a hint of forward progress was sensed and a cheer rose from the straining crowd he knew that maximum effort would have to be sustained to fully extricate the foolish lumbering vehicle.

He kept the straight six cylinders howling as the pickup-rope-bus ensemble slowly inched away from the roiling beach foam. With just the right revs maintained and the clutch held to semi-engagement they growled up the resistant sand. A disturbing burn smell of asbestos and rubber did not deter him even though he knew he was trading on the health of the '42.

As blue fumes rose around him Robin glimpsed a strange face in the jittering side mirror. Someone aged and not of this struggle stared back at him. He knew it was him but in its grave-eyed image he had the terrible revelation that this was a person he did not know.

Amid this skirmish with sand and tidewater it occurred to Robin that true life might not best be supported by such attachment to things. It was an odd revelation but compelling. Attachment, as he had been celebrating it for these past few years, solely meant grief.

More and more the mechanized shuddering began to create fear in him and then there came a legitimate gush of pure smoke from under the hood. He eased off the gas and set the brake. Pulling the transmission into neutral, he debated switching off the engine or perhaps letting it idle and circulate coolant to more evenly simmer down the various overwrought parts. He tried not to think of how destroyed the clutch pressure plates might be but was encouraged that there was no further fire.

Outside a cheering was rising as the bus backed up alongside and the driver jumped out. Hey man. That was superfine!

No problem. Make sure you get back up the beach. Tide's coming in fast.

No kidding. I'm out of here.

The crowd had the rope disconnected by the time Robin eased himself from behind the wheel. He slowly wound it around his arm and shoulder.

You are one righteous dude, man.

Hey that was fun let's do it again!

That was some kind of expert driving. Where'd you learn that?

Hot rod pickup. What a show!

Such a sweet little truck. Can we have a ride?

Hey are you going to Tofino? We need groceries.

My dad had one like this. We drove it off a cliff.

Do you sleep in there?

Did you drive this thing all the way from Regina?

He tried his best to be good-natured but found his fatigue to be sudden and all-encompassing. He bade temporary good-byes to all who stood around and slid back into the driver's seat and eased the truck into gear. The clutch was touchy but working as he slowly pulled back onto the impromptu highway that was the upper tide-line of the beach.

By the parking lot entry he slowed and once again surveyed the sand with an eye out for the particular vehicle he sought.

In minutes he paused a moment to examine a hefty Travelall and the glinting rounded trailer that had been the subject of such pride when last he'd seen it. On second regard he noted that the shine had come off considerably and the big tow vehicle had a serious rust-crusted gash in one of the fenders that in days past would have been repaired without delay. He pulled the '42 out of the wide thoroughfare and nestled it into a spot in the shadow of the Airstream. Though he did not expect a reception, every step of his way from the cab, through the camp, past the fire pit and random-strewn lawn chairs to the trailer door, he was ready to accept a greeting. None came. Even after he knocked twice on the bug-screened door.

Standing until uncomfortable and watching campers trudge by with sidelong glances, he saw a low car motoring past and he only understood it to be an unmarked RCMP cruiser when it slowed to a walk. Not wanting to know what it might do next he tried the door. Without the slightest creak it opened to a dark interior.

A scent of disinfectant tickled his nose, which then he understood was in fact some form of liquor. He let the door fall slowly closed without latching and waited for his eyes to adjust.

Dad?

There was no answer and no sound other than the ambient surf rumble outside.

Dad?

A rustle toward the other end of the trailer.

Dad?

He took two steps past the galley to the folding door of the bedroom and saw that it was not fully closed and when he drew it aside in the light of the louvered window there, underwear-clad, was his father lying diagonal across the double bed. By the fractured light of the semi-shuttered window Robin could see a whisker-stubbled chin and closed eyes.

When the eyes opened after a few seconds a slow recognition came. Is this a dream or are you —

I'm here, Dad. It's me.

The man shook his head and rolled to prop on one arm to take a solid look. Holy. Robin.

Yup.

But ... Where ...

I'm home now. Back from the prairies. Gonna go to school. Been looking for you.

Looking for me? Wha? Oh. Well. How's the farm? How's Jimmy? Did he pay you off? Get sick of you? I guess it was about time you came back.

Jimmy's dead, Dad.

Dead?

Cancer. I think he wrote you about it.

Well ... Yeah but.

It got worse and he died a couple of weeks ago.

His father coughed and rolled to a kneel to manoeuvre off the bed and stand aside Robin. Boy. You sure grew.

I guess.

And what's this? He nudged a knuckle to Robin's chin. Whiskers? We'll have to get you a shaving kit.

If you think. Robin swept his own hand across his face. I hadn't much noticed.

The elder turned and stepped through the open door of the washroom to splash his face. I can't believe Jimmy's dead.

I guess they told Mom but she didn't know how to contact you.

His father turned a bleary eye to him with hand-towel in hand. I would have found out eventually.

Well … sure.

Anyway. He pulled on jeans and buttoned a work shirt. Let's have a little breakfast and catch up. Last letter I saw was in spring when you finished Grade … what was it?

Nine.

Aha. So you're going into senior high.

Well not quite yet but … Next year.

Well good. Here. Go sit down and I'll get things going. He began assembling a stove-top coffee pot. And you saw your mother?

Yes. Robin cleared a spot aside the dinette and sat.

And Sebastian?

Yep.

They're doing okay?

Seems so.

Good. She's got things right in her head no problem. I left them plenty of cash too.

They're wondering when you're coming back.

Me? He paused amid pouring water from a pitcher on the counter into the bottom of the coffee pot. That's a good one.

It is?

Let's not talk about that right now. You want coffee?

Sure do.

Okay then. He poured copious water into the pot and laid a frying pan on the stove and pulled bacon and an egg carton from the refrigerator.

Their conversation during the cooking and the meal was mundane. At times there were uncomfortable silences. Robin despaired silently, not even as ravenous as he usually was when presented a welcome breakfast. When more time passed with empty conversation he'd had enough.

Dad … Robin leaned forward at the table and laid both elbows wide. What are you doing here? He forced himself to meet his father in the eyes and found it difficult.

Me? Reading books. Listening to the surf. Letting time go by. Like a human who needs a vacation. It's like … you know. You park a car for a time. Any car. Any perfectly good car or even one with problems. You park it and drive after a few weeks and it feels tighter. More efficient. Nicer to sit in and steer. Take a look at me. I'm an old car.

Robin snickered.

You're an agreeable kid now, Robin. And maybe you can comprehend some stuff. So I'll tell you. I've seen a lot and what I've seen pretty well convinces me there's nothing out there. Nothing once you're dead. He waved his fork for emphasis then placed a finger to his temple. It's all here and the important thing is right now. The truth. Once you get that through your head it kinda frees a fellow up for doing what he wants while he's alive. I mean. It doesn't have to be here. I half intended to go back out to the land myself. Look you and Jimmy up. Rove out over the old spread. You saw my dad's old place?

Yes. I drove out there. The house is pretty much gone but there's a shed or two. The crops came in good. Jimmy worked it until the sale went through.

Yeah the sale. I had to think on that one hard.

It's good land.

Yeah but there's no reason for a reasonable man to put up with living out there. Sure the crops come up when you plant them. Mostly. And the weather might let you bring in a profit two years out of three normally. But you know yourself. The dust will choke the breath out of you. The winter is long enough to make you forget there's any other season. Any place on the planet that requires a man to string a line from his front door to the outhouse so's when you gotta go you don't get lost in a blizzard. Or the pitch blackness of night where you can't see your feet on the ground. Isn't fit for human habitation.

Yeah. We had indoor plumbing, though.

Well. That's good at least.

They sat for more moments sipping coffee. Robin drummed fingers on the table. The town's dying, Dad. All the towns are.

I know. I can't go back. Sometimes I so wish I could.

The winters aren't so bad anymore.

Yeah I know.

But it's a hard go if you don't own the land outright. That's what Jimmy told me anyway.

Don't I know it. We got near half a million for those sections. Two years ago. This year you couldn't buy them back for twice that.

That's what I heard.

Man.

I liked it out there. Got to drive tractors and stuff.

You did, eh?

Yeah. I stopped biting my nails.

Did you? Well that was a good thing. Bad habit.

Yeah. It's too dirty to keep doing stupid stuff like that.

So you got to drive big machines, eh?

Jimmy saw that I got to know all the equipment. Had me rod weeding and swathing and combining. Dumping loads into granaries and all that.

How'd you do?

Fine. Except for one time. I weeded a whole forty acres one afternoon with a piece of rod broken off.

Oh?

Jimmy said it was all right. An honest mistake. Didn't seem to mind the strip of weeds.

Which field?

The one out front of the house. On the slope toward town.

His father plunked down his coffee cup with what sounded like a change of mood. Jimmy was a fearsome man when he drank. He'd drive drunk. Throw things around. His wife left him. Hands would quit and walk out on him.

I saw it.

This rod weeder screw-up. You do a thing like that it means more than a loss. It means all kinds of deep trouble. Jimmy wouldn't have worried about it or blamed you because he knew it was way beyond remedy. Way beyond fixing. A thing like that. All that effort. The fuel for hours operating. The time. The uselessness in trying to fix things up. But most of all the look of it. The green stripe running up and down his field. And the one on front of the house no less. The one running along the Glenbain Road off down the slope and as far as anybody cares to see. That would have been the worst part.

I know. It was bad.

See kid. It doesn't matter that you're a sweet child. Your mother loves you. You take good care of her and see that she gets what she needs by the way. You respect and treat everybody with kindness and generosity. Everybody knows you do that. You're a fine guy no question. But if you're part of a thing like this rod weeder foul-up it follows you.

I'm here now. That's why.

Part of the reason I got out of the prairies. And it was the sense too that unless a body tended to memories and living artifacts of a life they tend to fade and go away never found. So forget. Then there is no remembering. No matter how hard the synapse strain ... gone. To nothing. If you can live with it. Fine. If not. Work.

I don't know what all that means, Dad.

Yeah sorry. My mind kind of wanders. I did some acid a while back.

Whoa. I almost did too.

Don't you dare. Not yet anyway. Not until you've had a whole lot of experience.

I've had a whole lot of experience.

It shows. But that's not what I'm talking about.

What are you talking about?

The kind of thing that's nearly unmentionable.

Mention it.

Well. I guess it doesn't matter anymore. If you're going to get ruined in the head it'll likely have happened before now.

Robin gulped hard and tried not to show it. Nothing's ruined me.

Maybe not. We'll see. But I hope you can handle stuff that's coming. Do you remember when I was a volunteer firefighter?

Yup.

We went out on a call one time. Little kid had drowned in a swimming pool. Pitiful. To see the guys working on him with a machine. His mother sobbing off to one side. Small town. Everybody knew everybody so something like this didn't have distance. It was all so close by. Nobody could forget about it. This stays with you and it's not a good thing.

Both took long swallows of coffee.

Robin gulped again. The other night I heard this girl's last word.

How do you mean?

She'd gone through a windshield. Slammed against a tree in Cathedral Grove. I was with her when she died.

Jeez, kid ... A hard look across the table. So that's what's in your eyes. Well. If there's one thing I've learned. Just watch out who you're with when you die. If you can. Did she know what a good guy you are?

I don't know. I don't think she knew anything. I tried to talk to her.

Did she get comfort from that?

I sure hope so.

Man. You don't want it to be anybody who truly cares for you. It'd be a trauma for them. It's a good friend you need. Someone strong enough that you can be with and bear the terrible thing it is to die.

I guess so.

Life is pretty much just trying to get through without your heart turning to frozen stone.

I can see that.

And knowing that no matter what your intention you might not be able to help. Things will happen beyond your control. Tragedies. Awful injustices. But you won't be able to do anything about it. It's a bitch but there it is.

I guess.

Say. If you were in the grove overnight how did you get here? Hitchhike?

No.

Well I guess you got to Qualicum by train or plane. Did Jimmy's family take care of you that way?

No.

No? Well. How did you get out here then?

I drove.

What?

I know it's crazy but ... I drove.

But you're only ...

Just turned sixteen. Day before yesterday.

What? Oh. Is it —

August thirtieth.

Well.

It's okay. Mom already cooked me a birthday dinner and Seb gave me a good present.

Heh heh ... Well. So then you must have ... You didn't hitchhike here from the other side of the island?

Nope.

You could have. Everybody does.

I suppose.

Did you come through that big fire they were talking about?

Yep. I even stopped awhile and helped fight it.

You did, eh? That why you don't have hardly any eyebrows?

I guess.

Ha. Well. Good on ya.

Thanks.

So. You drove here?

Yep.

Without a licence.

So far, yeah.

In what?

It's parked out the side. Robin pointed past his father's shoulder at the curtained window.

Huh?

There was a quizzical look he remembered from his father's clowning accompaniment to the brothers' Saturday morning TV cartoon lineup. As he turned to part the fabric and take a look it occurred to Robin that there was also a note of angered fear in his father's manner.

No! Without pause his father rose from the banquette and made for the door faster than Robin anticipated. When he caught up his father was rounding the corner around the hitch assembly and widening his arms at the truck in a disbelieving awe. It's not the forty-two. It can't be!

It is.

The forty-two? He turned to peer squarely in Robin's face. Our old one?

Jimmy taught me to drive it the first day I was there. Said it was the one he and you drove first.

It is. It's the first vehicle I ever drove. And you got to learn on it too?

I used it the whole time. Robin's pride was florid now like he had never felt it before but with it came odd sentiment that stopped his breath and choked intended words. And brought it … out here.

Oh man. I'll bet that's quite a story. He walked alongside it and ran a hand along its lines. And she's not in bad shape either.

Jimmy kept it in a barn.

He did, did he? Yeah, that's old Jimmy. Was. What a guy.

I loved him, Dad.

Yeah … He stood by the driver's door and looked down.
That was the kind of guy he was.

They stood in a reverie of mechanized admiration mixed
with the wistful hopelessness of those who know they will
never do justice for the dead in any sense. Such was their momentary fixation that the roll-up of a police car made no immediate impact. It was the cutting of the engine and click of
the door that made them notice.

Good afternoon. A Royal Canadian Mounted Police corporal stood placing his hat upon head with two hands and
staring at them with stern concern. I wonder if you fellows
might identify yourselves for me.

Robin's father leaned against the '42 and rearranged his
expression. I'm Alvin Wallenco. This is my son Robin. Is there
a problem?

The officer stepped around the '42 and gestured to it with
a booklet in his hand. We have this vehicle as reported stolen.

What?

The corporal flipped pages and read. It was unlawfully removed from the property of a James Robertson Scott.

Well … Alvin spoke in measured tones but Robin knew by
innate experience that anger was rising. He sold this truck to me.

Mr. Scott is recently deceased, sir. And he left no indication
that he wanted to disburse it.

Whether he did or not is immaterial. This truck belongs
to me.

How is that sir?

Just look at the registration.

We have the registered owner as a Robin Wallenco. I believe
that's your son here. He's fifteen I understand?

Just turned sixteen. But he's not the owner of this truck. I
am.

How is that sir?

Just check my ID.

Your name is Robin Wallenco too?

That's right.

You told me your name was Alvin.

My middle name.

Can you prove it?

I'll go get you some ID. Alvin sped around one end of the trailer and away. Robin and the corporal stood uncomfortably.

When handed Alvin's driver's licence the policeman examined it carefully. So your full name is Alvaris Robinovitch Wallenco?

That's right.

The officer handed the licence back. And you're going to tell me that you were in Saskatchewan earlier this month and signed to register this vehicle?

I challenge you to prove I didn't.

We just might.

Go ahead.

If there is an irregularity here it'll likely carry a stiff penalty, sir. Obstruction of justice. Public mischief. That kind of thing.

We stand by what we say, Corporal.

We?

My son and I.

The policeman sighed and shook his head. Wouldn't it just be easier to admit that a mistake has been made? He head-gestured toward Robin and spoke directly to Alvin. Some kind of juvenile lark.

There's a man named Teller in Kincaid who'll back up this information. Alvin turned to his son. Isn't that right, boy?

Robin was jolted and impressed that his father remembered the name after so many years. Yup.

Alvin turned back to the corporal. Teller handles vehicle registration in the district. You want we get in touch with him right now?

You could show me the registration. We have it on the system indicating as you say. In the name of a Robin Wallenco.

His father turned to Robin and nodded toward the cab. Show the corporal the papers on this baby. Robin went to the glovebox and gathered them up.

Hmmm. The policeman noted the numbers on the form and wrote carefully in his notebook. We'll be looking into this. Meanwhile. He looked up at Robin and his father. Are you two residing as a family unit?

Each looked at the other.

Yes.

Robin stayed silent.

What can I record as your permanent address?

Robin and his father looked at each other.

That's a hard one, Corporal.

Is it not the place indicated on your driver's licence?

I've been meaning to get that changed.

You better. Or I'll have to write you up on that too.

Meanwhile. I don't think you have much on us.

You leave it to us to determine what we have on you. The corporal folded his notebook and wedged it into a shirt pocket. We'll do some checking. He moved to the driver's door of the cruiser.

You do that.

As the police car moved off down the beach father and son watched it silently amid the ocean rumble and chatter of beach walkers drifting by. His father patted the roof of the '42. We might not get to keep this baby.

I guess. Maybe we can talk to Cullen.

From what I remember he's a stubborn cuss. Like his dad.

Darn.

Anyway. Do you have the key on you?

Robin pulled it from a jeans pocket. We'll have to take it easy. I darn near burned the clutch out this morning.

His father's face hurt him.

It was for a good cause. I helped some people out of a jam.

There's lots of ways to help people without misusing machinery.

I know.

The requisite silence took the sting out of the remonstration and the huff out of the affront.

Okay then. Let's take her for a ride.

Thereupon came the sought moment of Robin's life that brought carefree breeze through his hair and a first utterly easy feeling in the passenger seat while as confident a driver as he'd ever known took the wheel and cruised them languidly up and down the broad shoreline. The brilliance of light against trees and buildings and cars from the high glare of the sun felt right. With light on his face and his father's grin and the looks of young girls as they passed he jubilated as he had never remembered and hoped and wished the essence of those miles down the long track would reside within him the whole rest of his life.

Dinner was an assemblage of what Alvin had in the fridge to be flung on a briquet barbecue. The fumes mingled with the fresh sea breeze. Robin found the combined aroma transformative and once in a while sensed a flavour he associated with the night so many few nights ago in company with Aldis.

A bottle of beer was handed to him. It went down better than any he'd ever had. He accepted a second as his father took his fourth, stirring a pot on the grill and flipping one-handed a mixed menu of burger and chicken wing. They ate and spoke little until Alvin's sixth bottle was near drained. He pushed his plate to the centre of the table and sat back on the couch. You know. It was better for everybody.

Yeah, Dad?

Yup. Your mother and I, we …

Robin let the pause go as long as comfort would allow. You what, Dad?

Oh. Never mind. You're a happy boy nowadays, aren't you?

Well. Yeah. I guess.

You guess. You're healthy, right?

Sure.

You got money.

Nope. Spent nearly the last bit of my paper route cash just getting here.

I mean through me. You've got money through me. Whatever you need.

Well that's good. I want to go to college.

What?

I keep running into people who tell me to. From what I've seen I agree with them. I'm thinking it might be a good idea.

You don't need more education. Our people got by fine with damn little learning.

Our people? You mean the prairie relatives?

Them. Us. Me and your mother. Common sense is all you need. And hard work.

I'm not afraid of work.

I can see that. The way you took to grain-spread chores. The way you tend to that truck. Alvin spread his arms wide. So you see? It's good as it is. You don't need any more school. In fact, you should forget about Grade Ten. Go get a job. They're always hiring at the mills. Or join a road crew. Or look into the railroad. There's plenty of things to work at without twiddling your thumbs in some classroom.

But Dad, you …

I what?

Don't … seem that happy.

How do you know how happy I am? What do you know about happiness anyway? Or anything, for that matter. You're just a kid. Act like one. You've been too big for yourself ever since you could walk. Trying to be more than you are. What's the matter with you?

There's nothing the matter with me.

Not for you to judge, little boy. Not for you to judge.

Alvin lurched upward on a course for the refrigerator. You just listen to me … He pulled open the cooler door and peered inside. We're out of beer. Too bad.

I don't mind.

Well I mind. Alvin stepped back and reached for a cupboard door. In a moment he had a near-full bottle of rye sitting on the counter and was washing out a glass from the sink. I mind a lot. You want some of this? He held the bottle toward Robin.

No thanks.

What's the matter? Too good to have a drink with your old man?

This beer has been fine. Before now I've never had more than one at a time.

Oh. So you think your old man is a drunk, eh? Think you're better than me. Better than all of us. Alvin poured a shot and watered it from the tap. Well I drink like a real man. He threw back the glassful and swallowed with a backward snap of his neck.

Dad. You don't have to do that.

I don't have to do what? Alvin spoke while pouring.

Drink to prove anything. I mean. I just want to sit around and talk, you know? I drove all this way pretty much just to see you.

You did, eh?

On the farm I got to know a lot of things. What happened out there. The stuff that happened to you. What your dad was like.

My dad? How could anybody know what that asshole was like?

Jimmy saw pretty much what was going on.

He didn't see half of it. Alvin tossed back his drink and poured another. Nobody did. 'Specially during the war.

Because he wasn't even around.

Because he wasn't even around. Alvin stumbled back to the couch, tumbler of whisky sloshing on his hand. And not all that much after, I'll tell you.

Anyway. I hoped maybe you and I could talk about it. I don't know a lot of the stuff that went on but I sure learned a lot about farming and machinery and stuff.

Well. Good for that at least. But you don't need to know anything else.

But Dad —

Don't you "but Dad" me ... Alvin slumped onto the couch. You must think you're pretty much a hotshot. All that brave driving over the prairie. Stupid thing to do.

No Dad. I just wanted to bring it over here to you.

You must think you're some ... Alvin's sneer and the quick drink he took while expressing it told Robin the conversation was coming to an end. Damn it. I thought all this stuff would blow over.

What stuff?

Aw nothing you can do about ... Never mind. Alvin slugged back the whisky in his glass.

There's no need to get upset, Dad.

How do you know what there is to get upset about? How do you know anything?

I just wanted to talk.

Okay. We talked.

I just hoped ...

Hope is for fools, boy.

Robin chose silence over any retort.

Alvin snarled to himself, stood wavering and stepped to the table. He poured more whisky and drank the undiluted liquor in a single draught. He poured another long shot and staggered to a slump on the couch. After a few minutes he snapped to: And that godawful truck out there. That's the only thing the bastard ever gave me.

I know, Dad. Jimmy told me. I guess that's why I made sure it got here.

Well it was dumb ... Stupid.

Robin again defaulted to a tacit participation. He looked to the floor and found it near impossible to direct his gaze anywhere else. Soon he was distracted by the sound of his father's snoring.

Alvin sat sleeping with chin against chest. Robin stepped lightly to his side and rescued a quarter-glass of rye as it was about to fall from the man's grip. He lifted his father's feet to lay him fully out on the couch and found a blanket to cover him. Then he went to the toilet to relieve the pressure of two bottles of beer, turned out the lights, and resumed his seat.

• • •

Robin woke with a start that hurt his neck. His father was gone. He rose stiffly from the chair to do a survey from the wide living room window. Out on the dark beach he could only see the remains of died-down campfires along the diminishing crescent.

A streak of moonlight shimmered across the water. Amidst his reverie Robin almost dismissed the significance of an inconsistent blob of black inside its perfect sheen. Then the actual shape of it impacted his consciousness.

What?

Unmistakeable to him was the understanding right now that the '42 was in the water.

He hurried through the door to run bootless in loose sand. On wetter stretches he got up some speed but it was still at least a minute and a half before he approached the growling pickup. Visible by the moon's illumination and flickering brake lights were gouts of watery sand being sent up by its spinning rear wheels.

Waterslosh at ankles then knees scarcely hindered Robin's splashy progress to wrench open the driver's door. In the dark he could only see the form of Alvin, slumped forward. Robin grasped and tugged with bare feet planted staunchly on either side of the running board. His father was speaking.

You're killing me. You're killing me.

Robin gripped his father's collar and yanked him bodily from the seat. Such was the force of his tug that Alvin's feet scarcely touched the running board as he plunged to the surf. Landing back-first in the roiling brine, Alvin immediately rolled to his feet to stumble forward, away from Robin and the stuck truck.

Robin slid behind the wheel just as the engine gurgled its last and a large wave slammed headlong into the grille and charged upward in a black sheet. The downwash rivered over and into the cowling vents. Robin could not blink his eyes or properly breathe. He gripped the wheel tight. He forced his right hand to disengage and punch the starter button. Nothing happened. He repeatedly punched and punched and punched and slumped hopeless against the wheel. The semi-immersed horn burbled balefully. This surprised him and renewed his efforts to get things running again, despite the seawater sluicing in on a fast-incoming tide. The starter button did not revive the submerged engine. Robin scarcely let himself deduce all the things wrong with the machine now as salt-foamy death encroached on the vehicle's electrical vitals.

Moments later a wave nudged the truck backward a little. The movement broke Robin's despair. He considered stepping out and trying to push it shoreward by himself and near cried at the absurdity of such an attempt. An anger rose.

He understood now that a phase of his life had passed and it was once again up to only him to move on. He groped for the new tool box his brother had given him. His hand touched it in the dark. He lifted it and slid from the driver's seat for what he knew was the last time. He even carefully shut the door behind him before plunging into the now stomach-high waves.

• • •

Starting from troubled sleep through a terrible night Robin opened his sticky eyes. There was direct sunlight in his face. Breeze rustling through nearby trees mingled with the distant rumble of surf. He lay inside a sand-moulded cozy beside a log that defended against any kind of wet wind, his head on the hard metal of the tool kit. He rose sore and sad and purposefully avoided looking out to the part of the beach — now low-tide exposed — where he supposed the '42 would be lying sandbound.

He found that though he had not overstressed himself during the previous days his muscles felt otherwise. He pulled up his jeans to amble the waterside, avoiding human contact where possible. A plan slinked itself vaguely into his mind: a walk to the Airstream; no dialogue with his father; simple acquisition of belongings — most of all his boots — then a hitchhike back to Mom's place.

The beach held its usual joy-spirited groups of long-haired prancing denizens. Robin was at least buoyed to know a cohort still existed that knew happiness without possessions or plans or commitments. Each time his bare foot penetrated sand he joyed to extract it from the suction back into the sun-drenched air. It was an oddly satisfying sensation. He even sought out the thin rolling suds at the top of the tide to run alongside the rushing water and kick up great mists of salt and sand. For some time people passed and bemusedly stared at the prancing youth with the heavy-looking red tool kit in his hand, kicking at the seething brine.

After an hour or so he tired of the silliness and headed for shore and a grim confrontation with his own despair. Walking with head down, purposefully not looking asea, he reached the logs and camps of the high tide line and turned toward his father's distant trailer.

Rounding a turn marked by a particularly tall stump lodged into the shoreline Robin was arrested by the sight of the '42 up on blocks. It was parked facing the shore and surrounded by a changing gang of intent wrench-holders and rag workers. Robin nearly stumbled. He glanced seaward to where he felt sure he'd left it stuck in the sand, turned back to look again and nearly sobbed aloud.

Hey cool, man. Where you been?

That's the guy! The guy who saved our bus yesterday.

Oh for sure.

This is his truck. Told ya.

Hey kid. What are you doing over there?

Robin looked away and back again to fully confirm that he had actually seen what his heart so wanted him to see. A familiar coterie of personalities stood intently gazing his way.

Come on over. I think we'll get her all fixed up for ya.

Whoa you must have been majorly ripped, man. She was nearly right under when we heard the horn.

Yeah good thinking. We just heard it. Got enough guys to come down and haul the thing back on the beach before it went under.

Robin strode to the truck, put his hand on the up-folded cowling, and peered downward into the dark engine compartment. He saw that the distributor cap had been removed and the spark plug leads were gone. Several men were working at a nearby bench, wire-brushing spark plugs and leads. A man in mechanic's coveralls with the longest hair he'd ever seen was blow-drying an ignition part with a can of compressed air. The driver's seat had been removed and an attractive girl was heating the cab interior with a whining hair dryer.

We're cleaning her out man.

Jason's Winnebago has a generator.

Been running all morning for Susie's hair dryer.

What possessed you, man? I mean by the looks of things the other day this baby means the world to you.

I didn't do it. My dad did.

Whoa … your dad? What the hell for?

He … He was drinking.

Booze, eh? Yeah. Figures. Nobody ever did a thing like this on weed.

It must have been more than being drunk.

It was … We had an argument.

And he took it out on this truck?

I think he might have been trying to kill himself.

Whoa … a suicide try?

Whatever for. Life is good, man.

Because he nearly killed me a bunch of years ago.

Heavy.

I was hoping he'd get over it. I don't think he has.

Wha'd he do? Ground you for a month? That'd kill me.

No.

Take away your *Playboys*?

Robin leaned against the truck and stared downward. A sob began to intrude on his composure and he knew in an instant that he needed to talk.

He was mad at me. I was late for dinner or something. Me and a friend had been straightening out wire coat hangers to make into hotdog-roasting sticks. We were gonna go on a camping trip. I had smoothed mine in a vice with no kinks. Nearly perfect. I sure was proud of it. I showed it to him and Mom and my brother. But Dad got this strange look on his face I'd never seen before and grabbed it and wound it around my neck.

Oh man.

Like tight, man? Like attempted-murder style?

Robin gulped, determined to continue. He was laughing the whole time. This weird angry laugh.

Diabolical, man.

Like, did you fight back or anything?

I was twelve. And I don't remember what happened after. I don't remember anything after he started doing it and my Mom and brother just sat and watched. My memory is a blank after that.

It's a wonder you survived, man.

Whoa!

Outrageous, man.

But I forgave him. I really did.

No reason in the world to do that to a kid.

He should be in jail, man.

Strange reaction to guilt if you ask me. Driving a truck into the surf.

He was drinking. I don't think he knew what he was doing. And if I hadn't got there in time he might have died.

Still.

I forgave him.

Well … The girl drying the cab stood and faced Robin directly. A person has to, Robin. He is your dad.

That's what I felt …

Oh man. Any guy who would strangle his kid …

He didn't mean to. He's sorry.

He better be.

Sorry's not good enough sometimes, man.

It's … It's not … He's …

Hey you don't have to talk about it if you don't want to, man.

Robin indeed could not believe he had spoken the words. He put the lapse down to the disparate emotions so recently bombarding him. Whatever the cause, he felt uneasy having so abruptly disclosed such a borehole in his soul.

He wandered around the work area and surveyed the operations as a way of moving on mentally from what he hoped was the lowest place he'd ever be.

But then something happened.

Robin stood again by the cowling and put his hand on it. The usual reassurance he'd taken from the very solidity of the machine was oddly absent in this moment. Instead he was more aware of the pleasant salt breeze, the warmth of the sun upon his face, the casual happiness of the comforting words issuing around him. Though logic told him he should have been elated at the miracle salvage of the '42, Robin could

summon only mild appreciation. He surmised that he had
by last night's terror and grief moved into an emotional region new and liberating. He no longer felt attached to this
machine. The feeling was a revelation to him. The '42 was an
admirable object, an extension of him, but it was not him.
The simple understanding of it all nearly made him chuckle.
A drug-like euphoria rose up. He took his hand away and
stepped back.

Someone handed him a breakfast of bread and tomato with
a cup full of beans. Quietly eating, sitting on a log watching, he
saw that he was not needed in the recovery effort and decided
to confront the inevitable. He set aside his plate and resumed
his trek toward the Airstream.

• • •

The emptiness of his father's trailer as he pulled on his boots
would in future years represent a metaphor for that time and
place. Without sentiment he gathered the rest of his gear and
did not search for any sign of the camp's permanent denizen.
Looking around, Robin understood that the vacancy inside was
a statement to him personally. With a nod of his head to no one
in particular he accepted what had happened and headed back
to the scene of the '42's resurrection.

The truck was off blocks when he arrived and the coverall man had just finished hooking up a new battery. Robin
peered at the engine with its shined-up wire leads and pristine
distributor cap now replaced and fully connected. The whole
compartment had been scoured to the point that one would
never know it had been immersed up to the top of the firewall
in seawater only half a day earlier.

I sure appreciate this, you guys.

Least we could do for saving the bus. It's our home, man.

Huh. Well this is kinda my home too.

We get you, man.

We had to borrow a battery from that broken-down Chrysler. The coverall man pointed to an abandoned-looking sedan parked just over the berm in the parking lot. Nobody's tried to start it for weeks. I think they just hitchhiked away and forgot about it.

Gee. I hate to think I'm stealing anything.

Naw, man. You needed a new unit, that's for sure. Yours was fried.

I guess.

If they come back we'll make sure we find another battery for them. Bound to be somebody around here with a spare.

I sure hope so.

Night approached during the beehive busyness of putting the '42 back together. Robin recovered his focus enough to immerse himself in work alongside the others. There were pretty girls on the work crew.

The girl who had worked in the cab brushed her chest against him while they were scrubbing and they exchanged smiles. Then memories of Aldis intruded and he felt odd. After another touch, though, when she handed him her hair dryer to dry some wires below the dash, his memories blurred.

Without even getting to know her name, Robin sought to sit beside the girl at the evening meal, their thighs in contact as both gazed into the fire. Beers were distributed and Robin was soon immersed into such welcome emotional oblivion that he was scarcely aware of another set of thighs close on the other side. He glanced to see that he was now snugly accompanied by the oldest man of the group, now out of coveralls.

How's your evening, friend?

Uh … Gee I can't thank you guys enough, uh …

Clement.

Clement. I can't believe how much work got done.

It was a fun thing to do.

Sure am grateful.

That's a good way to feel. Almost as fine as when you helped us down the beach.

Oh. That wasn't much.

You put in an effort that went long. Anyone could see that. And extra deep. They way you pushed your truck to do things it could barely do. The determination. It looked like you were near to trading your soul.

Huh. Yeah. I guess. I mean, that old thing can't take too much punishment. She might have died right there and then.

Precisely. That makes you a special man.

Thanks.

And it traces back through your life. An ethereal credit. You're like a superhuman with powers that exceed even your own understanding.

Robin let that one sit for a moment. Wow. Really think so?

I've met your type. Not often but yeah. I can see into you.

You can?

Not in a bad way.

How?

Have you ever done acid?

Nope.

I've spent much of the past year or so exploring it. Doors of perception. It's been a transformation.

What did you need to transform from?

I needed to get over some things and progress into other things.

Over things?

I was in the war.

Oh yeah?

Part of me remains there.

Okay.

I see in you the warrior that many of us tried to be.

You must have some stories.

Stories I will never tell. Memories I have struggled to keep at a distance. But never mind all that. Why are you here? And where are you going from here?

Oh. Well. I guess I'll finish school.

And after that?

College.

And then?

I don't know.

And along the way?

I don't know what you mean.

What does your spirit seek?

Ha ha ... You got me there. I don't think much about spirits or anything like that.

I predict you will, my friend. You will quite a lot. There will come a time you seek only your spirit. You will lose yourself in ethereal journey.

Oh?

Just like now. You come to us helping, but with injury in your soul.

Yeah, I ...

The story of your father. This makes things clear to me.

Clear?

And your joy in contact. The love you receive through even the lightest touches of dear Susie on your other side.

Is that what her name is?

Clement chuckled and gazed at the fire. You've got love-craze written all over your face.

I do?

It is a beautiful thing. But ...

But? But what?

Clement turned from the firelight and stared into Robin. Your pain. You are hurt.

Oh?

You are suffering whether you know it or not and there will be no cure for a long time.

Gee. You're kinda full of good news, aren't you?

I'm not saying you can't be happy. I'm sure you will be. You will be many good things and many you meet will be the better for it. But there is a long road.

Well. I got a truck to take it in.

Heh heh ... yes. But there is something else I sense. You have need of intense love in volume and whether consciously or otherwise, you will strive to obtain it. You will be obsessed. There will be victims in your path. Though you will always be an honourable person you will transgress against yourself.

Man. I don't know what to say.

Nothing. Finish your beer. Clement rose. Have another one. Get ready for the ride of the rest of your life.

• • •

Robin stayed fireside for as much of the evening as he could before sleep took him. He spoke to Susie beside him and he was gripped in an iron draw. Her physicality glowed as an electric-charged magnet force he knew he was helpless to. He was aware of how quickly he was forgetting Aldis.

Clement's prophesies bothered him. They were ominous and weird and such candid assessments of his character he could not help but feel an intrusion. But down deep in his alcohol-illusory current state of mind Robin knew that something about him was awry, at least as far as his pride in self-control was concerned. As he touched Susie he felt down to his atoms that he would irresistibly crave the ministrations of love. He would indeed give in to an irrepressible yen for the thrill of arms and breasts and vulvae. But especially the heart. He would seek and procure as much immersion as he possibly could, no matter the consequences. As he reasoned over the words Clement had spoken, Robin both cringed and chuckled to himself at the moist trueness of it all.

• • •

Morning light featured the '42 standing parked and gleaming though it was sometime after noon before Robin slid behind the steering wheel and noted a slight dampness beneath. The bench seat still bounced when he jounced upon it but there was a squishy element that would be there for some time.

Clement approached to pull up the cowling and gave Robin the sign to hit the starter.

There was coughing and catching and firing of black pops out the rear.

And then Robin had never heard such a welcome sound as the engine settled to a reassuring purr. Clement lowered the cowling and stepped back, tossing Robin a friendly salute.

After a few minutes Robin killed he engine and rummaged in the glove compartment to find the registration.

Out back he lowered the tailgate as the camp milled about. Clement stepped up wiping his hands with a rag. You sure about this?

With pen in hand and about to scribble Robin looked into his eyes. Pretty sure.

Okay.

You'll take care of her?

Of course. An honoured place will be made.

It's an … amaranth.

Huh. Weirdly, I know what that means.

A lady told me the word.

Eternal lady. Eternal pickup truck. It's all of a pattern, man. It's all of a world.

Kind of. Robin took one last long look at the rust-colour skin and glinting glass. And whoever takes it …

Don't think about that. If you're sure about this don't even think about it.

Robin bent to write upon the documents, then folded them and passed the small package to Clement. You might get hassled by the cops. Some people think it was stolen.

Either way.

I guess, eh?

Yup.

Clement shoved the paper into a back pocket.

• • •

They fashioned a backpack out of found sacks around the camp and designed it specially to accommodate the tool box. When fully loaded with the few clothes he'd brought, as well as water and a sandwich, Robin shouldered it and strode off the beach. Once or twice he glanced back to wave goodbye and caught a drop of moisture seep from an eye. He allowed that a tear would be appropriate to such a situation but he joyed that it was not a bitter one. His boots nearly mired in the loose sand at the exit point as if forbidding him to leave. He nonetheless slog-marched his way to the highway.

As he strode down the dusty coast road and stuck out a thumb, a kick of salt wind brushed the side of his face. It felt good for a moment and then the good was glee.

If the hitchhiking was what he was told it was he would be reaching a far shore before the sun was gone.

Acknowledgements

A good number of readers opined on this work over the years: Geoff Berner, Sheila Ross, Maxine Tobin, Sharon Stewart, Soressa Gardner, Simon Hearn; good friends and advisers all.

A particular tribute is owed to Betsy Symons and her Qualicum Beach writer's workshop; Donna, Charlie, and Pat.

> ... Style has work to do. It has to speak up for
> values the character could not express ... and
> for times not our time.
>
> —Denis Donoghue

I am grateful too to the Canada Council and British Columbia Arts Council.

About the Author

DENNIS E BOLEN has published six novels, two books of short fiction, and a poetry collection. A long-time veteran of creative writing workshops, he studied at the University of Victoria under Professors Robin Skelton and Lawrence Russell. Later, he earned an MFA at the University of British Columbia, concentrating on stage drama with Professor Brian Wade, and fiction with Professor George McWhirter. For several years he taught introductory creative writing at UBC.

In addition to a career as a federal parole officer in the Vancouver District, Mr. Bolen was fiction editor at *subTerrain* magazine for ten years. He also established himself as a widely read literary critic, writing for newspapers and magazines nationwide. He was a part-time editorial writer for the *Vancouver Sun* and a board member of a theatre group and literary festival.

After nearly forty years living and working in Vancouver and an unsatisfying attempt at life in a small town, Mr. Bolen moved with his wife, the electronic music composer Soressa Gardner, to a rambling Edwardian-age house in Victoria's James Bay neighbourhood. Mr. Bolen has famously — to his friends! — declared himself a lover of cities; one who could never live in a place without a jazz club.